"You don't need to be afraid of me, Charlotte."

"I—I'm not," she stuttered.

"I see the look in your eyes when I move toward you too quickly. I try to give you your space because I know that feeling inside your chest when terror grips your heart," he whispered, holding his hand near his chest. "It's all you can do to stop yourself from running."

"I'm not afraid of you, Mack. I just know it's smart to keep you at arm's length. I don't trust easily, but I trust you. That scares me more than anything."

"Because trusting me means I could hurt you?" Her head barely tipped in acknowledgment. "I wouldn't do that, Charlotte. I've been where you're at." He held up his hand to stem her words. "I mean that I've been hurt by the people who were supposed to look out for me. The feeling of betrayal is so powerful you can taste it. That's when you realize the only person you can trust is yourself. Am I close?"

THE RED RIVER SLAYER

KATIE METTNER

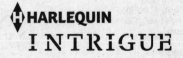

For my three Es

Thank you for always supporting and encouraging my work,
even when you have to admit to your friends that your mom
writes romance novels. I couldn't have asked for kinder, more
empathetic kids than you three, and I'm so proud to see you out
making a positive impact on the world.

H HARLEQUIN®
INTRIGUE™

Recycling programs
for this product may
not exist in your area.

ISBN-13: 978-1-335-59154-8

The Red River Slayer

Copyright © 2024 by Katie Mettner

All rights reserved. No part of this book may be used or reproduced in
any manner whatsoever without written permission except in the case of
brief quotations embodied in critical articles and reviews.

This is a work of fiction. Names, characters, places and incidents
are either the product of the author's imagination or are used fictitiously.
Any resemblance to actual persons, living or dead, businesses, companies,
events or locales is entirely coincidental.

For questions and comments about the quality of this book, please contact us
at CustomerService@Harlequin.com.

TM and ® are trademarks of Harlequin Enterprises ULC.

Harlequin Enterprises ULC
22 Adelaide St. West, 41st Floor
Toronto, Ontario M5H 4E3, Canada
www.Harlequin.com

Printed in Lithuania

MIX
Paper | Supporting
responsible forestry
FSC® C021394

Katie Mettner wears the title of "the only person to lose her leg after falling down the bunny hill" and loves decorating her prosthetic leg to fit the season. She lives in Northern Wisconsin with her own happily-ever-after and wishes for a dog now that her children are grown. Katie has an addiction to coffee and Twitter and a lessening aversion to Pinterest—now that she's quit trying to make the things she pins.

Books by Katie Mettner

Harlequin Intrigue

Secure One

Going Rogue in Red Rye County
The Perfect Witness
The Red River Slayer

Visit the Author Profile page at Harlequin.com.

CAST OF CHARACTERS

Mack Holbock—Mack is a haunted man, and sees his time at Secure One as a way to right wrongs he couldn't in the army. Now, someone is hunting women like the one he's been protecting, and he's primed to take him down.

Charlotte—She's been at Secure One for six months, healing from the trauma of sex trafficking. Can she step up and help Mack end the Red River Slayer's reign of terror?

Eric Newman—Has he outgrown Secure One or has Secure One outgrown him? Eric doesn't know, but he's tired of playing third fiddle.

Selina—The responsibility of caring for traumatized women is starting to take its toll on Secure One's medic. The truth keeps hitting too close to home.

Senator Chet Dorian—The senator from Minnesota is known for making enemies. This time, he needs Secure One to find an unknown one.

Eleanor Dorian—The daughter of Chet Dorian, she lives a sheltered life away from the politics of Washington, or so she thinks.

The Red River Slayer—The FBI can't find him, and he thinks he's safe. Until one of his victims lands on Secure One's doorstep. Run, run, as fast as you can...

Chapter One

They shouldn't be here. Mack Holbock had had that thought since they were first briefed on the mission. The hair on the back of his neck stood up, and he swiveled, his gun at his shoulder. The area around the small village was silent, but Mack could feel their presence. Despite what his commander said, the insurgents were there and ready to take out any American at any time. The commander should have given them more time for recon. Instead, he executed a mission on the word of someone too far away to know how the burned-out buildings hid those seeking to add to their body count. Mack knew the insurgents in this area better than anyone. He'd killed more than his fair share of them. They didn't give up or give in. They'd put a bullet in their own head before letting you capture them. If you didn't get them, they'd get you. Survival of the fittest, or in this case, survival of their leader maintaining his grip on terrorized villages.

That said, the first thing you learn in the army is never to question authority. You follow orders—end of story. No one wants your opinion, even if you have intel they don't have. His team had no choice but to go in. Mack still didn't like it. He didn't join the army by choice. Well, unless you consider the choice was either the military or prison. He *chose the army because if he had to go down, he would go down helping someone. In his opinion, that was better than being shivved in a prison shower.*

The kid with a chip on his shoulder standing in the courtroom that day was long gone. The army had made him a man in body, mind and spirit. He'd learned to contain his temper and use his anger for good, like protecting innocent villagers being terrorized by men who wanted to control the country with violence. As long as Mack and his team sucked in this fetid air, they had another think coming.

"Secure one, Charlie," a voice said over the walkie attached to his vest. His team leader, Cal, was inside with their linguist, Hannah. They needed information that only Hannah could get.

"Secure two, Mike," he said after depressing the button.

"Secure three, Romeo," came another voice.

Roman Jacobs, Cal's foster brother, was standing guard on the opposite side of the building. So far, all was quiet, but Mack couldn't help but feel it wouldn't stay that way. They needed to get out before someone dropped something from the air they couldn't dodge. He shrugged his shoulders to keep the back of his shirt from sticking to him as the sun beat down with unrelenting heat. The one hundred degrees temp felt like an inferno when weighed down with all the equipment and the flak jacket.

"Come on, come on," he hummed, aiming high and swinging his rifle right, then left of the adjacent buildings. There were so many places for a sniper to hide. He checked his watch. It had been ten minutes since Cal checked in and thirty minutes since Hannah had gone

into the complex. She would have to sweet talk some of the older and wiser women in the community to cough up the bad guys' location. Sharing that information would be bad for their health, but so was not rooting the guys out and ending their reign of terror. If Hannah could ascertain a location, their team would ensure they never showed up around these parts again. There was far too much desert to search if they didn't have a place to start.

"Charlie and Hotel on the move," Roman said. "Entering the complex veranda, headed to Mike."

"Ten-four," he answered before he backed up to the complex's entrance. With his rifle still at his shoulder, he swept the empty buildings in front of him, looking for movement.

A skitter of rocks. Mack's attention turned to a burned-out building on his right. A muzzle flashed, sending a bullet straight at the courtyard.

"Sniper! Get her down!" Mack yelled, bringing his rifle up just as another shot rang out. The "oof" from the complex hit him in the gut, but he aimed and fired, the macabre dance of the enemy as he collapsed in a heap of bones, satisfying to see.

"Charlie! Hotel!"

"Secure one, Charlie."

"Secure two, Romeo."

"Secure three, Echo."

"Mack!" Cal hissed his name, and it snapped him back to the present.

"Secure four, Mike," he said, using his call name for the team. His voice was shaky, and he hoped no one noticed. Not that they wouldn't understand. They'd all served together and they all came back from the war with memories they didn't want but couldn't get rid of. Sometimes, when the conditions were right, he couldn't stop them from intruding in the present.

At present, he was standing behind his boss, Cal Newfellow, dressed in fatigues and bulletproof vest. Was that overkill for security at a sweet sixteen birthday party? Not if the birthday girl's father was a sitting senator.

"Ya good, man?" Cal asked without turning.

"Ten-four," he said, even though his hands were still shaking. It was hard to fight back those memories when he had to stand behind Cal, the one who lost the most that day. "Something doesn't feel right, boss."

"What do you see?"

"I don't see anything, but I can feel it. My hair is standing up on the back of my neck. My gut says run."

"We're the security force. We can't run." Cal's voice was amused, but Mack noticed him bring his shoulders up to his ears for a moment. "Keep your eyes open and your head on a swivel. Treat it like any other job and stop thinking about the past."

Mack wished it were that simple. Cal knew that not thinking about the past was tricky when you'd seen the things they had over there. War was ugly, whether foreign or domestic, and Mack was glad to be done with that business. He liked the comforts of home, not to mention not having to kill people daily.

He glanced at his boots, where the metal bars across the toes reminded him that his losses over in that sandbox were his fault.

At least the loss that ended their army careers for good was his fault. Mack had missed a car bomb tucked away in the vehicle he was tasked with driving. He was carrying foreign dignitaries to a safe house that day, but nothing went as planned. In the end, Cal had lost most of his right hand, Eric had lost his hearing and Mack had suffered extensive nerve damage in his legs when the car bomb shot shrapnel across the sand. Now, the metal braces he wore around his legs and across his toes were the only thing that allowed him to walk and do his job. Something told him that tonight, he'd better concentrate on his job instead of worrying about the past.

"What are the weak points of the property?" Mack asked, fixing his hat to protect his ears better. It was early May, but that didn't mean it was warm in Minnesota. Especially at night in the rain. Sometimes working in damp clothes with temps hovering near forty-five was worse than working in ninety-degree heat.

Cal swept his arm out the length of the backyard. "The three hundred and fifty feet of shoreline. This cabin is remote, but anyone approaching from the road would be stopped by security. If someone wants to crash the party, it'll be via the water. We need to keep a tight leash on the shore."

A tight leash. That had been the story of Mack's life since he'd been four. His mother was the first to make helicopter parenting an Olympic sport. When his dad died in a car accident, and Mack survived, she became obsessed with keeping him safe. His mother would have kept him in a bubble were it possible, but she couldn't, so she kept the leash tight. Sports? Out of the question. He could get hurt, or worse, killed by a random baseball to the head! As much as Mack hated to say it, he was relieved when she'd passed of cancer when he was seventeen. She was more a keeper than a mother, and it had to be a terrible way to live. It wasn't until she was diagnosed with blood cancer when he was fourteen that she started living again. The sad truth was that she had to be dying to live. When she passed away after three years of making memories together, he was relieved not for himself but her. She was with her soulmate again, and he knew that was what she'd wanted since the day he'd passed. Mack was simply collateral damage.

When he was seventeen, he'd stood before a judge after breaking a guy's arm for talking trash about a female classmate. He was told there were better ways to defend people than with violence. If you asked him, the military personified using violence to defend people. He joined the army to find a brotherhood again. He'd found one in Cal, Roman, Eric and his other army brothers. They were Special Forces and went into battle willing to die to have their brothers' backs. Until the one time that he couldn't. It had taken Mack a long time to understand he shouldn't use the word *didn't* when it came to what happened that day when Cal's soulmate was taken before their eyes. It wasn't that he didn't. It was that he couldn't. His mind immediately slid down the rabbit hole toward the car full of people he didn't save. Mack shook his head to clear it. Going back there would result in losing sight of what they were doing here.

Mack eyed his friend of fifteen years and reminded himself that Hannah hadn't been Cal's soulmate. He used to think so, but then Cal met Marlise. Hannah had been a woman Cal loved in youth. Her death opened a path for Cal to start a successful security business and eventually find the woman who centered him. The moment Cal's and Marlise's eyes met while the bad guys bombarded them with bullets, time stood still. Cal used to think he started Secure One Security because of Hannah, but not anymore. They all believed Marlise was the reason. The tragedy that started years before was the catalyst to put Cal on that plane when Marlise needed him.

It had been three years now since they met. They were engaged one month and married the next, which hadn't surprised the team. Marlise had shown Cal that he could love again, but Mack never thought he'd see the day. Not after the scene that spread out before him in that court-yard. Then again, Cal never saw that scene. He never saw his girlfriend with a fatal shot to the head. He never had to drag his friend's body out of the square, stemming the blood oozing from his chest to keep him alive until help got there. Cal hadn't known any of that. It was Mack, Eric and Roman who lived that scene. They were left with the worst memories of a day when they could save one friend but not the other. Whether he liked it or not, Cal had been spared those images, and Mack was glad. There weren't many times you were spared the gruesome truth of war.

Not all wars are fought on foreign soil. The new team members of Secure One had taught him that three times over. Roman's wife and partner in the FBI had been under-cover in a house filled with women who had been sex traf-ficked and forced to work as escorts and drug mules. Mina had been injured to the point that she lost her leg and had come to work at Secure One when she married Roman. Their boss at the FBI, David Moore, was responsible for her injuries by putting her undercover in a house run by his wife, The Madame. Because of the deception, Roman and Mina could retire from the FBI with full benefits.

Marlise was one of The Madame's women in the house with Mina, and when she arrived at Secure One, she was broken and burned but determined. She wanted to help put The Madame behind bars. As she healed, Marlise worked her way up from kitchen manager to client coordinator, but not because she was Cal's girl. She had earned her position by observing, learning and caring about the people they were protecting.

His thoughts drifted to the other woman at Secure One who sought shelter there not long ago. About six months ago, Charlotte surrendered to Secure One under unusual circumstances. She was working for The Miss, the right-hand woman of The Madame in the same house Marlise and Mina had lived. The Miss had left Kansas and moved to Arizona to start her escort business, funded by drug trafficking. Charlotte was one of the women she took from Red Rye to help her. The Miss had made a mistake thinking Charlotte was devoted to her. She wasn't, and she wanted out. Last year, she'd helped them bring down The Miss by providing insider information they wouldn't have had any other way.

Charlotte took over the kitchen manager position when Marlise moved up to client coordinator and fit in well with the Secure One team. She had healed physically from the illness and injuries she'd suffered while living with The Miss, but her emotional and psychological injuries would take longer to scab over. She'd been homeless for years and then went to work for people who used and abused her without caring if she lived or died. There was a special kind of hell for people like that. Mack hoped The Miss had found her way there when he put a bullet in her chest.

Had he needed to kill her that night in the desert? Yes.

Her guards had had guns pointed at his team, and there was no way he would lose another friend to her evil. As it were, Marlise took a bullet trying to protect Cal. Thankfully, it had been a nonlethal shoulder wound.

On the other hand, the gaping chest wound he'd left The Miss with was quite lethal and well-deserved. Mack had learned to channel his temper in the army, but he couldn't pretend he wasn't angry at the atrocities that occurred in a country that was the home of the free to some, but not all. He would defend women like Charlotte until his final breath so they would have a voice.

Mack rolled his shoulders at the thought of the woman who currently sat in their mobile command center on the other side of the property. The mobile command center offered bunks, food and a hot shower to keep the men warm and fed when they were on jobs away from their home base of Secure One. A hot shower and warm food were on Mack's wish list at that moment.

The hot shower or seeing Charlotte again?

His groan echoed across the lake until it filtered back to his ears as a reminder that he didn't need to concern himself with the woman in the command center. He could protect her without falling for her. He noticed how his team raised a brow whenever he helped Char in the kitchen or took a walk with her. He didn't care what they thought. She needed practice in trusting someone again without worrying about being hurt. It was going to be a long hard road for her, so the way he saw it, he'd be the one to teach her that not all men were bad, evil or sick. Sure, he'd done some bad things, but it hadn't been out of evilness or demented pleasure. He had done bad things for good people in the name of justice or retribution, making the world a better place to live. She didn't need to know that, though.

His gaze traveled the lakeshore again, searching for oncoming lights and listening for outboard motors. It was silent other than the call of the loons. The hair on the back of his neck told him it wouldn't stay that way for long.

Chapter Two

"Charlotte?" Selina called from the front of the command center. "I need a break for a moment."

Charlotte stuck the pasta salad into the fridge and dried her hands before meeting Selina at the bank of computers in the front of the renovated RV. Cal had spared no expense when he'd gutted it to make it work for his business. Three bump-outs provided a large kitchen and bathroom, bunks in the back where six people could sleep at a time and a mobile command post to put the FBI to shame.

"What's up?" she asked the woman sitting at the computers.

"Hey," Selina said, motioning at the four screens in front of her. "Would you keep an eye on these for a few minutes? I need to use the restroom and get something to drink."

"Sure. I don't know what I'm looking for, but I'll hold down the chair."

Selina stood and patted her on the shoulder. "There's not much going on since the birthday girl is inside with her guests cutting the cake. Watch for anyone who isn't on the Secure One team or teenagers trying to sneak away." She pointed at a walkie-talkie on the table. "Radio someone if you see anything."

"Got it," she promised. "There's pasta salad in the fridge if you're hungry."

"I'm starving. I'll grab a bowl and bring it back up here. I know you don't like covering, but I gotta go," Selina said, hurrying to the bathroom while Charlotte chuckled.

The computers were intimidating, but Charlotte sat in the chair Selina had vacated and watched the screens, looking for interlopers as described. Selina was the nurse at Secure One, which meant she went on every mission as their med tech, but when she wasn't stitching wounds and handing out Advil, she was the team's eyes in the back of their heads. Selina had been trained as an operative when she joined Secure One and was as accurate with a 9mm as she was with an IV needle. Sometimes, Charlotte wondered if she covered for Wonder Woman when she needed a break because that's how pivotal Selina was to the team.

"Mike to mobile command." The walkie squawked with Mack's voice, and Charlotte nearly jumped out of her skin as she fumbled for it.

She had to take a deep breath before pushing the button to speak. Mack Holbock always had that effect on her. "This is Charlotte. Selina had to step away."

"Hey, Char, how's your evening?" Mack asked when she released the button. She wondered if he realized his voice softened whenever he addressed her. Probably not, and she shouldn't be taking notice either.

"Quiet as a church mouse in here. Did you need something?"

"Nope, it was just my check-in time. There's a clipboard to check off my nine p.m. call-in. Do you see it?"

Charlotte released the button and found the board he referred to, searching for his name and putting a check next to 9:00 p.m. "Done. It looks like you're due for a break in thirty."

"Negative. That's when the dance is going to pick up. I can't leave my post on the shoreline. I don't want guests wandering down and falling in the drink."

"Mack, you know how Cal feels about that stuff," Charlotte warned.

"What are you? My mother?" he asked, but she heard his lighthearted laughter that followed. "I'll clear it with Cal."

"Okay, be careful," she said, wishing her voice hadn't gone down to a whisper on the last two words.

"Ten-four, Char," he said, and the box fell silent.

Mack had been calling her Char since she'd arrived at Secure One last fall with her hat in her hand or rather her hands in the air. She had surrendered herself, hoping to gain immunity against The Miss the same way Marlise had when the Red Rye house burned. The night of the fire, she hadn't known Marlise wasn't going with them to the airport. Had she known that, Charlotte would have refused to go as well. Working for The Madame, and subsequently The Miss, had been demoralizing, scary and for some, downright deadly. When she saw Marlise escape their grasp, Charlotte had vowed to do the same if she ever got the chance.

That was the night she'd had her first interaction with Mack Holbock. It was the moment she realized she was safe, and they believed she hadn't been working for The Miss by choice. Exhaustion, fear and relief took over, and she had fallen apart right there in the little room where they'd been holding her. Mack had scooped her up and taken her to the med bay for treatment. She couldn't remember much about that time, but she remembered him. His presence, more than anything. He was smaller than Cal and Roman, but only in the height department. He was ripped, strong and capable regarding his work, but he was also kind, quiet and gentle when the occasion called for it.

When Cal, Marlise, Roman and Mina had left to find The Miss, Mack stayed behind for a few days to ensure everything ran smoothly. Initially, he was the only one who believed that she had no ulterior motive. She needed that unquestionable acceptance more than anyone understood.

"What did I miss?" Selina asked, carrying in a bowl of pasta salad with the fork halfway to her lips. Before Charlotte could answer, she was chewing, moaning and swallowing the first bite. "This is brilliant. Pepperoni and black olives?"

"And Italian dressing, to list a few." Charlotte laughed as she stood so Selina could sit.

"Seriously, you learned your lessons well from Marlise."

"I'm glad you enjoy it. To answer your question, Mack checked in for his nine p.m. but isn't going to take his break at nine thirty. The dance is about to start, and he doesn't want anyone wandering down to the water and falling in."

"That sounds like Mack," Selina agreed, setting the bowl down and jiggling the mouse. "Normally, Cal has a hardline about breaks, but this isn't a normal job, so I'm inclined to side with Mack."

"Same," Charlotte said, lounging on the back of the couch while she waited for one of the crew to come in looking for something to eat or drink. "It isn't every day that you're tasked with keeping one hundred teenagers safe when the birthday girl is a sitting senator's daughter."

"It's a little nerve-racking, not going to lie," Selina said before shoveling in more salad.

Charlotte kept her eyes on the screens in case she caught a glimpse of Mack. She liked watching him work, which might be weird, but it was true. When he was working, he moved with military precision, reminding her that he had fought his own battles in life. Some of those battles remained with him, she knew. He'd told her that in so many words one night as they worked together in the kitchen. She'd sensed that he didn't open up much about his time in the army, so she let him talk. While his stories weren't specific, his emotions were. He was struggling with the scars left from those battles as much as she was from hers. Maybe that was what made them immediate friends and easy companions. They understood each other on a level of unspoken atrocities and nightmare-riddled dreams.

Charlotte had only slept those first few nights at Secure One because Selina gave her medication to keep her calm. After that, she slept in fits and bursts. Her psyche struggled to know if the people surrounding her could be trusted, and it took her several months to feel comfortable enough to sleep through the night, at least as through the night as she could when plagued by nightmares of men's hands holding her down. Mack always seemed to materialize in the kitchen at 2:00 a.m. on those nights when she couldn't close her eyes again. He'd sit by the butcher-block counter and share cookies and milk with her rather than scold her about not going back to bed.

"You know it's okay if you want to date Mack," Selina said.

Charlotte's brain came to a full stop and nearly slung her backward off the couch. "Excuse me, what now?"

"I said it's okay if you—"

"I heard what you said, but what makes you think I want to date Mack?" Charlotte had forced the words through a too-dry throat, hoping it sounded genuine.

"Because you like each other, which is obvious. Everyone else tiptoes around you two like sleeping lions, but I'm all about calling it as I see it."

"Clearly," Charlotte said, tongue in cheek. "I don't want to date Mack, but I'm happy to know it would be okay if I did."

"If you say so," Selina answered in a singsong voice that was a bit juvenile as far as Charlotte was concerned.

"We're just friends, Selina. First of all, he's five years older than I am."

"Cal is five years older than Marlise."

Charlotte chose to ignore her. "Second of all, I'm not ready to date anyone. Since working for The Madame, I don't know how to date. I don't know how to be with a man who didn't pay for my company."

"Do you trust Mack?" Selina asked with her back to her now as she watched the screens.

"You know I do, with my life, but that's different."

"I understand what you're saying, Charlotte. You're scared. I get it. I know you don't know me or my past, but suffice it to say that I do understand being afraid to rock the boat. I just thought you should hear from someone on the team that moving on and living your life now that The Madame is in prison and The Miss is dead isn't rocking the boat. You earned your freedom, and you should enjoy it."

The woman who had nursed her back to health fell silent then, and Charlotte stared at the screens as she considered what Selina had said. She had earned her freedom from The Miss and had been pivotal in helping them find her and rescue the other women. She could leave Secure One whenever she was ready, Cal had told her, but he'd also said he wasn't putting an end date on her employment. As long as she wanted to be part of Secure One, the team would welcome her with open arms. They had, which was the reason she wouldn't rock the boat. If she had to leave Secure One and find work in a different city with a different company, she could end up back on the street. That was the very last place she wanted to be.

The man in question walked onto the screen, and Charlotte watched as he made his way down the bank and disappeared from view. She turned away and walked back to the kitchen. Secure One was her life, and while Mack might be part of it professionally, that was as far as it would go. For Charlotte, self-preservation would win out every time, even if that meant being alone for the rest of her life.

THE CABIN OF Senator Ron Dorian was well hidden among the trees until they parted for a view of the Mississippi River. The *cabin* was a six-bedroom, four-bath summer home with a grand staircase and wall-to-wall windows in the family room that looked out over the water. Mack wondered how ostentatious his DC house must be if he called this his *cabin*. Then again, that wasn't his job. His job was to keep a young girl and her friends safe while they were on the grounds celebrating a milestone. Secure One had been in charge of the security on this cabin for six years, and they'd run point on plenty of parties held here. His worry at tonight's party? The sun had set, and one hundred teenagers were ready to pour out onto a dance floor under a rented tent. There was a 100 percent chance a couple or six would sneak down to the river to make out. Having one of them fall in the drink and get swept downstream was not the reputation Secure One wanted.

He'd been patrolling the football field length of shoreline for the last three hours other than the ten-minute break he'd taken inside the command center to grab dry clothes, boots and a snack. He hoped the rest of the crew didn't eat all the pasta salad before he got back there. It was one of the best salads he'd ever had, and that was saying a lot, considering Marlise used to be the resident chef. When he'd tried to compliment Charlotte on it, she'd turned away and acted like she hadn't heard him. He knew she'd heard him when her lips tipped up a hair before she spun away. She'd been fine when he'd done his 9:00 p.m. check-in, so he couldn't help but wonder what had happened in the meantime.

Mack went over everything he'd said to her the last week and couldn't think of anything that would have upset her. Maybe she was just having a rough night. Security at these events required a lot of planning, and even tighter control, which put everyone on edge. She'd be fine once they returned to Secure One and were back in the swing of their usual duties. At least he hoped she would be. Mack didn't like the idea that someone had upset Charlotte, especially if it had been him. Before Charlotte arrived, he'd taken the time to listen to and observe Marlise during her two years at Secure One. He'd understood that women in their situation had a hard time trusting people and had limited, if any, self-esteem. That led to difficulty staying employed or in school, often leading them back to the streets. He didn't want that for Charlotte.

She reminded him a lot of Marlise though. Strong, determined and seeking a better life. Charlotte had been that way since they'd hauled her in off the shoreline the first night. She'd wanted to escape the woman holding her captive and was willing to risk getting shot. Unlike Marlise, Charlotte's scars weren't visible. They were buried deep in her mind and soul, and she rarely let them show. A few months ago, she'd been sketching on her pad when he walked into the kitchen for a snack. She was a skilled artist and had already helped Secure One clients by drafting plans to provide specific problem areas with better security. That night though, her drawing drew his eye immediately. She'd tried to hide it from him, but he hadn't allowed it. His eyes closed for a beat when he thought about it.

The drawing was of a naked woman with bleeding wounds, tears on her face and vulnerability in every pencil stroke. She told him it was a self-portrait of how she felt inside. The slashes across her body and blood pooling by her feet would rest in his mind for always—most especially the wound to her leg where The Miss had buried a tracker not meant for humans. Despite Selina's best efforts, Charlotte had gotten an infection and now had nerve damage in the leg. She'd sketched an intricate tattoo around the scar that spelled out *worthless,* and he'd assured her she was anything but that. Those were just words though, and Mack knew women like Charlotte didn't believe wo—

A scream pelted the air in a high-pitched frenzy that relayed fear in a way Mack had heard only a few times in his life. He started running toward the sound just a few hundred feet ahead. He stopped in front of two teenage girls, no longer screaming, just staring at the water with their mouths open in terror. One girl had her arm pointed out with her finger shaking as Mack followed it to the shore below.

"Secure two, Mike. I need help on the shore, stat!" He turned the girls away from the water just as Eric came running from the other direction.

"What's going on?" he huffed, and Mack flicked his eyes to the water. Eric's gaze followed, and his muffled curse told Mack he'd seen her too. "I'll take them to the command center while you call the cops. We'll need to keep these two separated from the rest of the group until then."

"After that, get the party shut down while I deal with this," Mack hissed, and with a nod, Eric led the two women toward the command center.

Mack walked down to the lakeshore, holding his gun doublehanded as he navigated the rocks and wet sand. What could first be mistaken for floating garbage, on a second glance, was a woman with her long blond hair floating over her red dress. When he stopped along the shore to stare down at her, the woman's eyes were wide open, and her mouth made an *O* as though whatever she saw in the last moments of her life were welcoming her into the new world.

"What do you have?" Cal asked as he came running up behind Mack.

"Young woman. No visible COD. We need to get her out before she floats downstream."

"Cops aren't going to want us to touch her," Cal said as Mack holstered his gun.

"They're going to like trying to find her again in the Mississippi much less." Mack snapped on a pair of gloves he'd pulled from his vest and then grabbed his telescoping gaff hook. Everyone had one on their belt when they worked on the water. You might have to pull a fellow team member out of the drink at any time.

"We need a tarp before you pull her out," Cal said quickly, stopping Mack's arm.

"You'd better get one then," Mack growled and shook his boss's arm loose. "I'm going to hook her dress just to hold her here. If I don't, she's going downstream."

Cal hit the button on his vest that connected him to command central. "Secure one, Charlie. I need a tarp or plastic on the shore directly below the dance tent."

"What size?" Mack heard Selina ask.

"Body size," Cal answered, and it ran a shiver down Mack's spine.

Now secured by his hook, the young woman wasn't going anywhere, but Mack couldn't take his eyes off her. She couldn't be twenty-five, and her long blond hair reminded him of Marlise and Charlotte. He prayed that someone was missing this woman, and she wasn't the victim of The Red River Slayer. His cynical side said the slayer was responsible for this woman's death, and he was only getting started.

Chapter Three

The muted light through the window told her the sun was setting. She knelt by the bed and scratched another line into the wood. It was the five hundred and fiftieth. She knew some were missing from the early days when fear kept her huddled on the bed for most of the day. That was before she realized he wouldn't kill her. Now she marked the end of each day rather than the beginning of a new one. She suspected her end would come at night.

Frustration filled the woman as she stood. She had to get out, but the room was a beautifully decorated and posh fortress. She had all the comforts of home except for a way to contact the outside world. She also didn't have a television or a radio. She'd been *his* captive for too long. Soon she'd be replaced with a new plaything. That was how it worked. What he did with his old playthings, she didn't know. Probably sold them or killed them.

The thought ran a shiver down her spine. She hoped he'd kill her. The last thing she wanted was to be sold to another man in another country. If she had a way to do it, she would kill herself just to steal his joy, but he made sure there were no weapons for her to use. Who was he? She had no idea, but he had money, and he must have power. You don't keep women locked away in the basement of your home for years without the ability to make people look the other way. Then again, she had no idea if anyone lived in this house other than her. Maybe he just came to visit her or lived alone upstairs. In the early days, she'd tried to ask questions but soon learned he wasn't interested in answering them. Her fingers played across the puckered scar on her cheek. The night she pushed him too far with her questions, he showed her rather than told her to stop.

Her gaze drifted to the window above her bed. She'd tried to break it until she realized it wasn't glass. It was layers of plexiglass that no amount of pounding would break. She paused. Were those footsteps?

She moved to the door quietly on practiced tiptoes to listen. He should be bringing her dinner soon. He would sit with her while she ate and engage her in conversation that would be considered mundane in a different time and place. He stayed to ensure she didn't try to hide the utensils or kill herself with them. When she finished eating, he'd want her to thank him for dinner if he were in the right mood. She learned early on to obey that order, or she'd spend a week drinking her food through a straw until the swelling in her face receded from his beating. Oh, sure, he'd always apologize for hurting her and bring her ice and medicine, but he wasn't sorry. He thrived on the power he held over her, and beating her turned him on.

The footsteps stopped at the door, and a key jingled. She was back on her bed as the door swung open, and her monster walked through with a tray balanced on his arm. He was wearing his full leather hood and his smoking jacket tonight. He always wore the mask, but the smoking jacket meant she'd have to thank him properly tonight. Initially, she had nightmares about the mask, but after a few months, she found a way to ignore it and imagine the man behind the mask. She came up with ways she would take him down if she ever escaped.

He set the tray down on the bed and ran a finger down her cheek. She forced herself not to recoil. "Good evening, my angel. Little Daddy brought you dinner. Are you hungry?"

"Yes, Little Daddy," she obediently said while trying hard not to roll her eyes. She stopped being scared of him months ago, but she'd learned if she didn't want a backhand, she'd best comply with his demented fantasies.

"This will be one of our last meals together, angel."

Her breath hitched in her chest. This was it. She had to act tonight.

"Soon, you'll go to your new home with your new daddy. He can't wait to meet you. I'll miss you, but you're ready for him now. Are you ready for a new daddy, angel?" he asked as he set up the food on the table.

She nodded but knew she was out of time. This was it. It was time to put her plan into action. She'd spent months earning his trust, and tonight, she'd thank him properly for all the things he'd given her, but more so for the things he'd taken away.

"How long until the cops get here?" Mack asked Cal as they stood in front of the body. They'd laid her on the shoreline on a tarp, but they didn't cover the body for fear of contaminating it more than it already was.

"At least another thirty minutes," Cal answered while he fielded questions from the rest of the team as they sent kids home with their parents.

Selina was caring for the two girls who had discovered the body. They would wait at mobile command until their parents arrived. The police would need to speak with them, but Mack had no doubt their parents would want to be present.

"Who are we kidding?" Mack muttered. "The tumble she took down the Mississippi left no evidence of her killer for us to find."

"Us?" Cal asked with a brow up in the air. "There is no us. This is for the cops to figure out."

"And they've done a smashing job with the other three bodies they've found in the last few months."

The authorities had pulled three women from three different rivers over the last six months. The first woman had been found in The Red River and was wearing a red dress, which was how this particular serial killer had earned his moniker.

"Not my monkey," Cal said again. "We can't get involved in this, Mack. We have enough on our plates at Secure One."

"We've been involved in this since the day you brought Marlise onto the compound," Mack reminded him. "If this is yet another nameless, background-less woman like Marlise or Charlotte, that means someone is buying and killing women from the street. How long are we going to brush it under the carpet before we *get involved*?"

Cal whirled around and stuck his finger in Mack's chest. "Don't."

"Don't what, Cal?" Mack knew challenging his boss was risky, but they were also brothers, and sometimes you had to call your own family on their crap.

"Don't accuse me of inviting this into our lives. That was not what I did when Marlise came to Secure One."

Mack held up his hands in defense. "That's not at all what I was saying, Cal. I simply meant that we're taking care of women just like this one," he said, motioning at the woman behind him, "while others are still dying. The cops are missing something. How long will we stand by without at least trying to prevent more deaths?"

Cal shook his head and planted a hand on his hip. "Mack, I wish there were a way to get involved in this case, but there isn't. The FBI is involved and—"

"The FBI can't find their way out of a paper bag!" Mack exclaimed.

"I don't disagree," Cal said with a smirk, "but we still can't go traipsing in like the *Mod Squad* and take over their investigation."

Mack snorted. "The *Mod Squad*. Okay, Grandpa, but I'm tired of women dying because of our inaction."

"Same," Cal said with a sigh. "In each victim, I see Marlise or Charlotte. It was just chance they made it out of The Miss's grasp alive. These poor women."

"All of them," Mack agreed.

As a man, he hated that some men thought they could use a woman and then throw her away like garbage. It enraged him to the point of violence, which didn't solve anything. The only way to stop it was for someone to figure out who was doing it. Unfortunately, Cal was right. With the feds involved, they couldn't be. Cal had been read the riot act after The Miss fiasco when he went rogue, and the woman ended up dead because of it. In the end, it was brushed under the carpet as a problem solved, but Secure One had to tread lightly whenever the feds were around. They didn't like their tiny toes stepped on.

"Secure two, Sierra."

"Secure one, Mike. Go ahead."

"Charlotte is on her way down," Selina said over the comm unit in his ear.

"What?"

"I said Charlotte is on her way down."

"No, don't let her leave the mobile center. She doesn't belong down here."

"Already tried that, Mack. You've met the woman, right?"

"I'll have Eric intercept her. Thanks for the heads-up."

Mack huffed as he grabbed his radio to call Eric. Of course, Charlotte would try to come down here. She felt responsible for these women as much as Marlise did. If Marlise weren't back at Secure One with Mina working the other client security, she'd be down here too. "Secure two, Mike," he said and waited for Eric to reply. Once he did, Mack explained the situation and signed off.

"You're not going to pass me off on someone else, Mack Holbock," a voice said from his left, and he spun in the dark without drawing his weapon. He knew it was her, even if he was frustrated by her inability to follow orders. He secretly loved that she still had some fight left in her. She didn't back down on something she believed in, regardless of what she'd been through in life, even if that personality trait made his job harder.

He stepped to the side enough to hide the woman on the ground, and Cal moved alongside him. "You shouldn't be here, Charlotte," Cal said firmly. "This is a crime scene."

She stopped and stood before them with her hand on her hip. Mack had to bite his tongue to keep from smiling. "I'm not contaminating your crime scene," she said, throwing around air quotes. "The Mississippi is contaminating your crime scene."

"What do you need, Char?" Mack asked, softening his voice as he took a step toward her. She needed to be on her way before she saw the body and realized she was a victim of the same nameless, faceless perp.

"I need to see the body."

"Not happening," Cal said, crossing his arms over his chest. "No one views the body without the police here."

"When the police get here, it will be too late. They'll bungle it the way they always do, and more women will die."

"More women will die? We don't know how this woman died," Mack reminded her.

Charlotte rolled her eyes so hard that Mack couldn't stop the smile from lifting his lips. "She's the fourth woman found dead in a river in six months. More women will die if we don't find the killer, Mack."

Mack turned and lifted a brow of *I told you so* at Cal before turning back to the woman in front of him. "Be that as it may, we must follow protocol, Charlotte. Protocol says we have to wait for the authorities."

"Are you going to tell them?" she asked, both hands on her hips.

"I won't put you through it. I know you want to help, but you can't."

"Don't tell me what I can and can't do, Mack," she hissed, standing chest to chest with him.

Cal's grunt was loud to Mack's ear, and he grimaced. His boss wasn't happy. Cal's flashlight snapped on, and he lifted it to Charlotte's chest. "It's not up to us, Charlotte—"

Her gasp was loud enough to stop him midsentence. His flashlight had illuminated the woman's head by accident, and Charlotte's eyes were pinned on her. Mack grasped her shoulder to turn her, but she fought him.

"I know her," she whispered, dropping to her knee on the muddy shore. "I know her, Mack."

Mack knelt on both knees, not caring that the cold mud soaked through his pants. He cared that someone on his team could identify this woman. "Char, how do you know her?" He could see shock kicking in, and he wanted the answer before she couldn't speak.

Cal switched the light off, and it went dark again just as Charlotte reached her hand out toward the body. "That's Layla."

"Layla who?" Cal asked as Mack put his arm around Charlotte. She was starting to shiver, whether from the cold or trauma, he couldn't say.

"I don't know," she whispered. "I met her in Arizona when I worked for The Miss. She was from one of the small towns around Tucson."

"Wait, she was with The Miss?" Cal asked from behind them to clarify.

Char nodded but dropped her gaze to the ground now that the body was in the shadows. "Layla wasn't there very long. She cried nonstop and cowered in the corner whenever The Miss came around. We woke up one morning, and she was gone. We figured she tried to run, and The Miss killed her. That or she got away."

"Would it be safe to say you met her two years ago?" Mack asked, trying to get some kind of timeline to help the police when they arrived.

Charlotte turned to him with wide eyes as she nodded.

"Something like that. Where has she been all this time, Mack?" She grabbed tightly to his coat when she asked, her face just inches from his now.

"I don't know, but now that we know who she is, maybe we can find out."

Charlotte shuddered, and Mack wrapped his arms around her as he glanced up at Cal and mouthed, "Don't tell the cops."

Cal tipped his head for a moment in confusion, but after a long stare, he cleared his throat. "Mack, please walk Charlotte back to the command center. I'll wait here for the police."

With a nod, he helped Charlotte up the grassy hill toward the lights shining in the distance. "I want you to listen to me, Char," he whispered, and she nodded. "Don't tell anyone outside of Secure One that you know the victim."

She tripped on her next step, and Mack steadied her as she lifted her gaze to his. "But, Mack, they have to find her killer!"

"Shh," he said, hushing her immediately. "First, the police will have to decide if she was murdered."

"You know she was!"

His finger against her lips muffled her exclamation. "We know she was, but the cops must *prove* she was. Does that make sense?" She nodded against his finger, and he lowered his hand and started walking with her again. "While they're busy proving she was murdered and searching for her identity, we'll be after her killer."

"But I already know who she is, Mack. If I don't tell them, I'll be in trouble when they find out I knew her."

He squeezed her to him to quiet her again. "You will

tell them as soon as they release her image to the press. That won't happen until they determine her cause of death. The same as they have with the other women found dead with no identity, though in this case, they may be able to get her identity if she wasn't washed like you and the women from The Madame's ring."

"That's true," she agreed with a nod. "She was a street girl but had a record, at least according to her."

"Good, good. Then the police will find out who she is without you telling them. When they do, you'll call to tell them you knew her for a few days and the dates she was with The Miss. That's as far as your responsibility goes with this case."

She stopped abruptly, and he caught himself from falling at the last second. "Wouldn't it save time if we could give them her identity tonight?"

"It would," Mack agreed, lowering his head closer to hers so no one overheard them, "but then we have no time to look into it at Secure One."

"But this sicko is out there hurting other women!" she exclaimed, and his finger returned to her lips.

"He's following a pattern. One woman every six weeks, at least that's been the frequency they've been finding the bodies. We can take a couple of days to try and track down the last knowns on this woman before we turn what we know over to the police. We're trying to prevent another woman from dying by helping the police, not working against them, okay?"

"Why do you think you can help now? Just because you have a name?"

He turned her and started walking toward the command center again. He wanted to get back before the cops showed up so he could hear what Cal told them. "This is the first time we've had the name of the victim, which means it's the first time we can put Mina on the task of following her trail before she disappeared. All we needed was one mistake from this guy, and he may have just made it."

"Killing a woman with an identity?"

"Killing a woman with an identity and leaving her where Secure One could find her. Our record speaks for itself regarding getting justice for women being held against their will."

A smile lifted Charlotte's lips, and he squeezed her shoulders one more time before reaching the steps to the command center. "It's safe to say Secure One has done better than the police, that's for sure," she agreed.

"Then trust us, just one more time, and we'll get justice for women like Layla too."

A shadow crossed her face, but it was gone before he could grasp its meaning. He had shadows of his own that he kept hidden, and he wouldn't judge her for hers. When she leaned in close to him, her scent of apple blossoms filled his senses, and he inhaled deeply. He reminded himself that he had no business liking this woman for any reason other than to keep her safe while on a job. At the mere thought, he laughed at himself. As if that were the only reason he liked Charlotte.

"Isn't it illegal to withhold information?" she whispered, so close to him that he could bury his nose in her neck and fill his head with her. He didn't, but it took every ounce of willpower not to.

"As far as the police know, only four people have seen the body, and only two up close—me and Cal. That's all they need to know. Right?"

She nodded once, zipped her lips and tossed away the key. Then she climbed the steps and disappeared inside the trailer. Mack couldn't keep the smile off his lips as he turned on his heel and walked back toward the shore in awe of the woman half his size with twice his strength.

Chapter Four

Charlotte approached the two girls who sat huddled together on the couch. Selina had covered them with a warm blanket and calmed them down so they could speak rather than just stutter words. Their names were Tia and Leticia, and they told Charlotte and Selina they were best friends.

She handed each girl a mug of hot cocoa and sat across from them on a chair. She'd seen a lot of horrible things on the street, and she remembered her reaction to the first dead body in a dark alley on the streets of Phoenix. Nothing prepared a person for that, and nothing could wipe the image away.

"Your parents are on their way to be with you until the police arrive," Selina said, hanging up her phone. "They're about ten minutes away."

"Okay, thank you," Leticia said before scooting closer to her friend. "What are the police going to ask us?"

"Basic questions," Selina assured them. "Your name and address, how long you've been friends with Eleanor Dorian, if you've ever been here before and what you were doing by the water tonight. It will be simple questions that you can answer easily. They know you didn't have anything to do with the woman's death. They just want to know if you remember anything that might be helpful to their investigation."

"Can we stay together?" Tia asked.

"That I don't know," Selina admitted. "It will be up to the police and how they decide to question you. You don't have anything to hide, so don't worry about it."

The girls glanced at each other again, and Charlotte noticed the fear that hid in their eyes. "What were you doing down by the water tonight?"

Another shared glance confirmed for Charlotte that they were hiding something they didn't want to come out.

"Girls, if you were drinking or smoking down there, the police will find out, so you may as well be honest," Selina said without judgment.

Tia shook her head and held her hands out to them. "No, no, we weren't. We'll do a test to prove it. We weren't doing that."

"Then you have nothing to worry about," Selina said again.

"Are you in a relationship together?" Charlotte asked, the truth evident.

"You can't tell our parents," Tia hissed, tears springing to her eyes. "Please."

Her protective arm around Leticia suddenly made more sense, especially when she pulled her closer. "We just wanted to dance together," Leticia whispered, "so we went down the hill where no one would see us. We aren't out because of my parents."

Selina knelt in front of them and rested her hands on their knees. "We aren't going to tell your parents. Let's take a minute to agree on what you'll tell the police if you're separated. You'll want your answers to match."

"You mean you'll help us hide the truth? Won't you get in trouble?" Tia's gaze flicked between the two women, and Charlotte took her other hand instinctively.

"There's nothing wrong with saying you went down the hill to escape the noise or see the river at night. Technically, that's what you did, right?" Charlotte asked, and they nodded.

"We danced and then walked out on the fancy lookout dock just as the moon came out from behind the clouds. The moonbeam on the water was magical and something you don't see living in the city, you know?" Tia asked, and both she and Selina nodded.

"Were there any boats on the water tonight?" Selina asked. It didn't surprise Charlotte that Selina would dig for more information when the opportunity presented itself. When she walked in the door earlier, Selina was already on the phone with Cal.

"No," Leticia said without hesitation. "All I heard was the rain falling on the water. I turned to kiss Tia, and that's when I saw the flash of red over her shoulder. When we focused on it, we realized it was a dress, and someone was still in it. She was floating down the river as though it were a sunny summer afternoon." They both shuddered again, and new tears sprang to Leticia's eyes.

"Okay," Selina said quickly, squeezing their knees. "Just tell the police that you were turning to go when you noticed the red dress." They both nodded robotically, and Selina glanced at Charlotte for a moment. "Did you see anyone else on the bank of the river? Anyone walking or running through the trees?"

"No, we didn't see anything, but it was so dark it would

have been hard. We wouldn't have heard footsteps with the music playing for the dance."

Selina patted their knees and then stood. "I just ran you through the questions the police will ask. Do you think you can handle it now?"

Both girls nodded, and smiles lifted their lips. "Yes, thank you," Tia whispered. "Thank you for understanding why we don't want to tell the police why we were down there."

"We understand you're in love, and that's a wonderful feeling," Charlotte said, leaning forward to talk to the girls. "Don't let what happened tonight steal that joy from you. Finish high school and then go to college where you can be together without worry. Life is hard, but love makes it worth it. Okay?" They nodded again, and Charlotte stood. "Want a refill?" She pointed at their empty mugs of cocoa and smiled as they handed them to her.

Charlotte disappeared into the kitchen to refill their mugs as her words flooded her head. *Being in love is a wonderful feeling.* She'd never been in love but hoped one day she'd find someone who understood her scars and loved her anyway. She ladled the sweet milk into the mugs and sighed. That was a tall order for anyone. Her mind's eye flicked to Mack tonight and the way he tried to protect her from the ugliness of life. She immediately shook it away. She wasn't here to fall in love with Mack Holbock. She was here to feed him and, if she had her way, heal him, so he could go out and find someone worthy of his love.

THE BRANCHES TUGGED at her skin, leaving red welts across her bare arms as she barreled through the dark, cold night.

She'd bested her *Little Daddy* and escaped the prison she'd been in for over eighteen months. She'd found an old pair of shoes by the door and a jacket, but with no phone and no money, she wasn't sure how she would find help. She was surprised how remote the house was when she tore out of the basement like the hounds of hell were on her heels.

She was tired but knew she had to keep going. How far was far enough? She didn't know. She'd been following the river, so she had to run into a town eventually, right? She had to find a car and get far, far away from wherever her current hell was.

Streetlights glowed in the distance, and she slowed to a walk. She had two choices: run past the town while it was still dark and keep going or stop and see what the town had to offer. Her first problem was a lack of money or identification. Her second problem was figuring out if The Miss was still in business without landing on someone's radar who would call the cops. She glanced down at herself and sighed. Her cami and boy shorts would land her on someone's radar, and she couldn't risk the cops finding her or alerting The Miss.

Think, she told herself. *You're in a forest with trees and a river. That means you aren't in the desert anymore.* The thought lifted her head, and she saw the town with fresh eyes. She was a long way away from Arizona. If The Miss was still doing business, she'd need long tentacles to know she'd escaped.

The idea spurred her forward into the shadows. First things first—clothes and then transportation. Ahead was a service station. No lights were on, which meant it was closed or shut down. A glance up and down the dark asphalt showed no cars, and she skittered across the road before sliding behind the brick building. She said a silent prayer as she dug in her coat pocket for the flashlight she'd found earlier. She'd been too afraid to use it before, but the risk was worth it now. Keeping it low to the ground, she searched the area behind the garage. A hulking metal body sat as a sentry next to the building. Focusing the weak beam of light on the license plate told her the first thing she needed to know.

Pennsylvania.

A long way from home, Toto, she thought. She didn't know the town's name, but it didn't matter. She wouldn't be there long. Sliding along the side of the truck, she noticed there was no logo on the side. That meant if she could get it started, it could be her salvation. A glance in the back of the rusty truck bed revealed old coveralls that she balled up under her arm for later. Hot-wiring a truck this old would be a piece of cake as long as the door was unlocked. She needed to get in fast if it was, especially if the dome light came on. With a steady breath, she pulled up on the truck's handle and prayed she'd caught her first big break.

It HAD BEEN hours since Mack had pulled Layla onto shore, but the property was still buzzing with activity. The police were interviewing kids as their parents looked on in horror, and the ERT team was on the scene looking for any evidence they could pull in and analyze. It didn't take a genius to realize there wouldn't be much left on the body after being in the Mississippi. The medical examiner gave them a time of death between seventy-two and ninety-six hours ago. Whether it was three days or four didn't matter. Trace evidence would have been washed away in the

Mississippi within minutes. That was the way The Red River Slayer wanted it.

Mack suspected they wouldn't find any labels in her dress, which would match the MO of the other women they'd found. Even if they could track down the dress, it would likely be from a big box store and sold in every state. The Red River Slayer had repeatedly proven that he wasn't stupid or careless. Mack hoped killing Layla was the perp's first mistake.

When working with the feds—correction, when the feds are running a case—you had to be careful that you don't tamper with evidence. Mack knew that, but before they arrived, he'd felt it was essential to check for vitals, which was why with a gloved hand, he had palpated her neck. He couldn't help that while he was doing that, he noticed petechiae in her eyes and her swollen tongue. While there were no ligature marks on her neck, that didn't rule out strangulation. It was surprisingly easy to strangle someone to death without leaving a mark. Mack would know. The feds were selling the cause of death as drowning, but no one at Secure One was buying. The person killing these women wanted to be hands-on, even if it meant holding them under the water while they struggled. That said, neither Mack nor Cal believed that to be the case.

It was more likely the killer felt these women needed to be beautiful even after their death, which was why they were placed in the river wearing red gowns. The Red River Slayer was helping these women find a better afterlife, whether from their past lives or what they had to do while they were with him.

For the first time, Secure One may have finally got some solid information about the guy. Since Charlotte knew Layla disappeared around eighteen months ago, and the ME put her time of death around three days ago, the math told him the perp kept the women for a long time. To do that, he had to have a home or building to house them without raising suspicions. It was a huge risk to hold someone hostage that long, which meant wherever he was keeping them had to be isolated with no neighbors or regular deliveries. Then again, maybe he kept them bound and gagged when he wasn't home. The idea of it sent a shiver down Mack's spine.

He was itching to return to Secure One headquarters so they could plot all their information on Layla against the other victims of The Red River Slayer. They may not be actively involved in solving this case, but that was the very basis of the Secure One team in the army. They were a ghost team that went in and got the job done. It was starting to look like they would have to do the same this time if they were going to stop this guy.

"Who's in charge here?" The man's brusque tone put Mack on guard immediately. He stepped up next to Cal as the man, nearly fifty yards away, was yelling. "I demand to know what is going on here!"

"Ah, yes, we knew it was only a matter of time before Senator Dorian arrived," Cal said out of the corner of his mouth. "Should we pass him off to the cops or try to pacify him first?"

"Let's take him back to mobile command. We can keep him occupied by walking him through the entire party while the feds do their thing here. I'm sure the feds will want to talk to him, but since he wasn't here to celebrate his daughter's birthday, I might add, there isn't much information he can give them."

"Agreed," Cal said before stepping toward the man to head him off. Mack followed, breaking right of Cal so they could turn Dorian toward mobile command. "Senator Dorian."

"Cal Newfellow! What is this I hear about a dead woman on my property?"

The senator was shouting now, which was unnecessary with their proximity, so Cal took his shoulder and kept him walking toward the motor home. "Sir, let's go to our command center, and we can show you what occurred this evening. Everything was recorded."

"I want to see this woman!"

"Not possible," Mack said as he quickly texted Selina with one word, incoming, before he finished answering. "The ME has already removed the body. We should talk inside."

They'd managed to herd the senator and his protection detail to the command center quickly and efficiently without drawing too much attention to him. The door opened, and Selina stepped out, holding the door for their entourage to enter. Dorian motioned for his team to stay outside, so Selina closed the door behind them.

"Where's Charlotte?" Mack asked her under his breath. The last thing he wanted was for her to overhear them.

"She's overseeing the kids waiting for a ride at the house. I didn't want her here just in case."

Mack nodded, glad Selina had anticipated this situation and acted accordingly. Senator Dorian was difficult on a good day. Tonight, he was going to be impossible.

"What is going on?" Dorian asked, raising his voice again.

"Settle down, Senator," Cal said, motioning with his

hands. There were few people Dorian let order him around, but Cal was one of them.

"You'd better start talking, Newfellow. I pay you to keep my name out of the news, not plaster me across the front page!"

"Senator, we cannot control where a body floats to shore," Cal reminded him. "All we can do is control what happens if that situation arises, which is what we've done."

"It was him, wasn't it? The Red River Slayer?"

A shiver went through Mack when he said the name. He didn't know who the guy was, but he was ruthless, and too many women were paying the price.

"We don't know that, Senator. People drown in the Mississippi all the time. We can't jump to conclusions," Cal reminded him.

"Nice try, Newfellow. Do you have any idea how bad this is going to look for my reelection campaign? I can't host a party here now!"

"Why not?" Mack asked with his arms across his chest and feet spread. He wanted the senator to know they wouldn't back down to his demands.

"Why not? Do you think anyone will want to come here for a party when there's a killer on the loose?"

Dorian's voice was way too loud for the small space, and Mack took another step toward him. "If the woman was murdered, it didn't happen here. The ME put her time of death closer to three to four days ago. While it was unfortunate that she washed up on your shoreline, no one is at risk of being killed here. For any future campaign parties you may host, we'll be here with more staff to protect the property from the road, the woods and the shoreline as we always do. There's nothing to worry about, Senator."

The tension in the room was taut, and Mack steeled himself for the tongue-lashing from the man, but it never came. His shoulders slumped, and he wiped his hand across his forehead before he planted it on his hip. "I'm sorry. I was terrified something had happened to Eleanor, and then to find out another young woman had died riled me up. They have to stop this guy."

"We're all in agreement about that," Cal assured him, directing him to a chair in front of the computer monitors. "Let's go over the footage from tonight. Maybe you'll spot something we overlooked."

Cal started the camera replay and lifted a brow at Mack from behind the senator. Mack bit back his chuckle. They didn't miss anything, and he was confident they'd played the entire night by the book. None of that mattered unless the senator believed it as well. The last thing Secure One needed was Dorian bad-mouthing them all over the country. Cal would do anything to make sure that didn't happen.

Chapter Five

"When will my dad get here?" Eleanor asked in a huff.

"He's chatting with Cal and the team now, so I'm sure he will be here soon, Eleanor," Charlotte answered, trying to placate her.

"Chatting," she said with an eye roll. "More like yelling and throwing his name around."

Eric's snort from across the room drove Charlotte to glare at him.

"What? She clearly knows her father." He gave her the palms out, and this time it was Eleanor who giggle-snorted.

"I also know Cal doesn't let my dad push him around. I'm glad about that. You should always stand your ground with bullies."

"You're saying your father is a bully?" Charlotte asked.

"Just calling a spade a spade. My dad thinks he's president of the United States already. He hasn't even run yet."

"Is he planning to?" Eric asked, leaning forward.

"Last I heard," Eleanor said with boredom. "It's all he talks about right now. I'm sure that's what he's planning to reveal at the next party. He needs big bucks to throw his hat in the ring, which means he needs big donors to like him."

Charlotte didn't follow politics, much less Minnesota

politics, but she would do a deep dive once they got back to Secure One. Dorian was a long-time client of theirs, and she wanted to familiarize herself with him, his career and his family. Well, his family was easy. He was a single father to Eleanor and spent most of his time in Washington while his daughter lived in Minnesota with his mother. Her grandmother raised Eleanor while Dorian pursued his career. Eleanor's mother was killed in a car crash when she was a baby, and Dorian had never remarried. Eric shot Charlotte a look before he picked up the tablet and started typing. He was probably making notes since the team was busy with Dorian in the command center.

"Why can't I go to my room?" The girl was frustrated, and Charlotte couldn't blame her.

"I'm sorry, Eleanor. Cal wants you to stay here with us until they're done briefing your dad on what happened tonight. I'm sure it won't be much longer."

"Please, call me Ella. Eleanor makes me feel so..." She motioned her hand around in the air until Charlotte answered.

"Old?"

Ella pointed at her. "Ancient."

"I understand," Charlotte assured her with a chuckle. "I feel the same way about the name Charlotte."

"I don't think Charlotte is a bad name, but maybe a little old-fashioned. Do you have a nickname?"

"I used to," Charlotte said, pausing on the last word.

"Well, what is it?"

"I've only told one other person this before." She paused, and Ella cocked her head, fully engaged with her now. Charlotte didn't want to lose that connection, so she took a deep breath and spoke. "Hope. I was an artist in my former life."

"You're still an artist. A damn good one," Eric said without lifting his head from the tablet.

That made both Charlotte and Ella smile. "I'm still an artist, but I was a street artist back then. Do you know what that is?"

"Sure," Ella said with a shrug. "You tagged buildings. Graffiti."

"I guess some would call it graffiti, but I painted murals on buildings while everyone else slept. They were my way of bringing hope to the other kids on the streets."

"Your tag name was Hope?"

Charlotte nodded, trying to force a smile to her lips, but it didn't come. She noted Eric nodded his head once as though he respected her. No one had ever respected her before, but that was the feeling she got from him and Ella. She could change her name to what it was before The Madame washed her history, but doing that meant she'd have to face her past as Hope. After all, there was a reason she'd jumped on The Madame's offer to change her name and find a new life. She just hadn't expected that new life to be as an escort, drug mule and mercenary against her will.

"That's a cool story. You must be a fantastic artist if you painted murals on buildings."

"She is," Eric said, still without lifting his head. "Charlotte—Hope—should show you some of her work. She doesn't just draw a picture. She tells a story. She has natural talent, and that can't be learned."

"Would you show me?" Ella asked with excitement. "I do some drawing, but I'm not that good."

"Yet," Charlotte said with a wink. "We all get better with practice and time. I don't have my sketchbook here, but I promise to bring it to the next party. We can hang out in mobile command and draw."

"That would be great," Ella said with excitement, but Charlotte also noted a hint of relief in her voice. "I hate his parties. He makes me show my face for a little bit, but then I always find a place to hide to avoid all those people."

"I feel your pain," Eric said, lowering the tablet. "There's nothing worse than a bunch of snobby adults jockeying for the top spot as richest in the room."

Ella laughed while she pointed at Eric. "I like you. Not many people get what it's like to deal with politicians and their donors. It's exhausting. That's why I live in St. Paul with my grandma. I want to go to school and live a normal life. Well, as normal as possible. Yes, I have to go to private school, but I could never live in Washington, DC, year-round. I go in the summer, and that's enough for me."

"I'm ex-army," Eric said. "I know what it's like to deal with the government and politicians. I don't blame you for wanting time away from that three-ring circus."

Eric's phone rang, and he held up his finger, then answered it, stepping into the corner of the room to talk to the caller.

Ella glanced at him and then leaned in closer to Charlotte. "I'm not kidding here when I say I need to go to the bathroom in my room or I'm going to ruin this gown."

"Understood," Charlotte said with a nod. "Let me get Eric."

"He's busy. Besides, I don't want him ushering me to my room to get pads. Please."

Charlotte could see Ella was embarrassed, but she bit

her lip with nervousness. They weren't supposed to leave the room on Cal's orders. Then again, he didn't put them in a room with a bathroom either, so she had to assume he knew they'd have to leave for that.

"Okay. This place is crawling with cops. It won't be a big deal to run up there, but I need to tell Eric, and I'm going with you. To your room and back. No other stops."

Ella held up her hands in agreement, so Charlotte walked over to Eric and leaned in to whisper. "She needs the restroom. It's an emergency. I'll take her there and bring her right back. Will Cal object?"

Eric put his hand over the receiver, glanced at Ella and back to her. "Not much we can do other than be careful. There are cops everywhere but stay alert. I'm not expecting any other problems tonight though."

Charlotte nodded and tucked her required Secure One Taser into the holster on her belt. While she was trained on handling a gun, she rarely carried one. Too many innocent people had died from a bullet meant for someone else, and she couldn't live with herself if she were the cause of an innocent person's death.

She motioned for Eleanor to follow her to the door. This was her chance to prove to Cal that she was part of the team, whether she was cooking for them or doing unexpected bodyguard duty on a US senator's daughter. Cal had trained her for this, and when she'd asked him why, his answer was simple: *You never know when you will have to keep yourself or someone else safe in this business. If you work here, you're part of the team, and everyone on the team does this training.* She always thought she'd never need it, but tonight, she was ready to prove she'd learned her lessons well.

CHARLOTTE STOOD OUTSIDE the bathroom door and waited for Ella. She had agreed to let her change clothes before they went back to where Eric was waiting. She was right, it didn't make sense to parade around in a ball gown, but Charlotte also didn't want to be gone too long.

"Hey, Hope," Ella called from inside the bathroom. Charlotte didn't cringe at the name, and that surprised her. "Did you happen to see Tia and Leticia before they left?"

"I did," Charlotte said, reminding herself not to spill their secret. "They left with their parents after they talked to the cops."

"Were they okay?" she called back through the door, and Charlotte heard rustling on the other side as though she were hanging up the gown.

"They were fine. Why?"

"They found a dead woman in the river. I figured they'd be shaken."

The door opened, and Ella stepped out wearing a pair of pajama pants and a long T-shirt. She was ready for bed, and honestly, so was Charlotte, but she dragged a smile to her face and nodded. "They were shaken up, but by the time they left, they'd calmed down."

"I felt so bad when I found out they were the ones who found her," Ella said, following Charlotte to the door.

"Why?" A look left and then right had Charlotte stepping out into the hallway with Ella.

"They go through enough already. It's hard being in the closet. Then, when you finally get some time alone, that happens."

"Wait. You know?" Charlotte asked.

"Everyone knows," Ella said with an eye roll. "We go

to a Catholic school, so we all pretend we don't know just to protect them."

"Wow, I wasn't expecting that."

"Why? Because I'm a snobby rich kid who doesn't care about anyone else?"

Charlotte stopped and spun on her heel to face her. "I would never think that, Ella. I've known you barely an hour and know you're nothing like your father. You care about getting to know people. I wasn't expecting you to say that because the girls told us no one else knew."

Ella's shrug was simple. "That's what they need to believe, so as a class, we decided we would let them believe it. We protect them whenever someone starts asking too many questions and always make sure we have parties where there's a place for them to escape together. Did you see them together?" Charlotte nodded but didn't say anything. "Then you know that they've already found their soulmate at sixteen."

Charlotte turned and started back down the hallway, keeping Ella on the inside of her against the wall. "Do you believe in soulmates?"

"I do. I think that's why my dad has never remarried. My mom was his, and when she died, a piece of him did too. He never dated again after she died. Women try, trust me, but he's not interested. I wish he would though."

"Why?"

"It might chill him out a little. He's always wound so tightly that I'm afraid he'll have a heart attack one day."

"I agree with you. Your dad strikes me as an all-work-and-no-play kind of guy."

"He so is, but this summer, when I'm in Washington, I'm going to do something about it."

Charlotte had already messaged Eric to let him know they were on their way back, and as they started down the stairs, she noticed that the house had cleared out and was much quieter.

"What are you going to do about it? Set him up?"

"That's exactly what I'm going to do!" Ella said, laughter filling the stairwell as they stepped onto the lavish parquet flooring. Calling this house a "cabin" insulted the artists who'd poured their souls into it. The view during the day must be breathtaking from the large bay windows that faced the back of it, and the chef's kitchen and extensive library weren't something you saw in most "cabins" in Minnesota. Charlotte hadn't lived in Minnesota long, but she did know that much.

"I'm sure that'll go over well," Charlotte said with a chuckle just as a man dressed in black stepped out of a hallway and grasped Ella's elbow.

"I'll take Miss Dorian to her father now. Thank you for your help," he said, tugging Ella's arm to follow him.

Charlotte instinctively grabbed Ella's other arm and held tight. "I need to see ID, and I'll have to call my boss before I can relinquish Miss Dorian into your care." She sounded calm, but she wasn't. She was panicking, so she forced the sensation back and focused on her training. *If you ever feel like something is off, hit your all-call button, and we'll come running.*

Mack's words ran through her head, but she hesitated, taking stock of the man again. He wore a black suit and coat, a black hat and had an earpiece running from his jacket to his ear. The tall man kept his head bent low, ensuring that Charlotte couldn't get a good look at him.

"I said, I need to see your ID."

"I'm protection detail for Senator Dorian," he repeated. "I don't have to show you anything."

"Then you can't take Miss Dorian. We'll wait for her father in the designated area. Come on, Ella."

Charlotte tugged on Ella's arm, but the man didn't release her. The girl looked terrified, which told Charlotte that she had never seen this man before. Without hesitation, Charlotte hit the button on her vest and then took hold of Ella with both hands. "You should leave now unless you have ID."

She unhooked the button on her holster, but she never got to pull the Taser before a fist flew at her from her right. She dodged it but not before it glanced off her jaw and tossed her head to the side. She didn't let go of Ella, who was now screaming for someone to help them. Charlotte couldn't worry about help arriving. She had to concentrate on protecting Ella. She was afraid he would punch Ella next, so she yanked the girl to the left and then kicked out with her right leg, landing a hit in the guy's solar plexus. He let out a huff, but it wasn't enough to stop him from hitting her dead in the eye with a sharp jab.

Ella had fallen to the floor and was crab-walking backward as the man went for her. Gathering her wits, Charlotte struck him in the back with her elbow and then hit him behind the knees with a back kick that sent him to the floor. Commotion and shouting filled the house as men came running from all doors, but the man in black wasn't giving up. He turned and swept Charlotte's feet out from under her, and she fell, hitting the floor with her head. Dazed, she knew she had to fight him off long enough for Mack or Eric to get to them. All she could think to do was lift her feet and kick up. A smile lifted her lips when the resounding crack told her she'd made contact with her target. He bellowed and pinwheeled backward, right into Eric's waiting arms, who quickly subdued him.

Charlotte didn't get up off the floor. She just stared at the cathedral ceiling, the colors swirling and spinning in the atmosphere around her. She had to catch her breath before she could move again. The fight had taken everything out of her.

"Hope!" Ella said, her face swimming in her line of sight. "Are you okay?"

Charlotte wanted to answer her, but all she could do was watch the swirling colors above her head.

"Hope, I mean, Charlotte needs help!" Ella yelled. Charlotte could hear the frantic tone of her voice and reached for her, trying to reassure her, but her hand missed its target and fell back to the hardwood floor. "Someone, please, help her!"

A voice broke through the din in the room, and she begged her mind to focus on the sound. It was her name on Mack's lips as he scooped her up, wrapped her in his protective arms and started running.

"I need a medic!" Charlotte found his bellowing voice more soothing than scary. "I'm going to get you help, Charlotte," he promised, and it was only then that she closed her eyes.

MACK PACED ACROSS the floor of mobile command, where the team had met up after the attempted kidnapping of Dorian's daughter. They'd have lost Ella tonight if it hadn't been for Charlotte. What had Eric been thinking letting them go alone? He would never say it to the man, he felt bad enough, but Charlotte had paid a heavy price.

"I'm fine, Mack," she said from the corner chair where she sat with an ice pack on her face. Not only did she have a concussion from hitting her head on the floor, but the jerk had given her a black eye and swollen jaw.

"You're a warrior, Charlotte, but I can't stop thinking about how close we came to a kidnapping on our watch."

"Me neither," she said, wincing when she held the ice to her eye. "Did anyone get anything out of the guy?"

All eyes were on Cal and Eric. They'd taken the guy aside and had a "chat" with him before the police arrived. "Not much," Cal said with a shake of his head. "I have to hand it to you. You broke the guy's jaw with that last kick. He was twice your size and strength."

"He wasn't taking Ella on my watch. When she looked at me with terror, I knew she didn't know the guy, which meant he wasn't part of the senator's detail. I had to stop him long enough for you guys to wade in and help me."

"I'm proud of you, Charlotte. Hand-to-hand isn't easy for anyone, especially when you're outsized the way you were. That was Secure One protection at its finest."

Mack noticed her chest puff up and her shoulders straighten at Cal's words.

"He's right, Charlotte. You saved Ella, and all of us here know it." Mack glanced at Eric, who was glaring at them with his arms crossed over his chest. Whether he was ticked at them or himself, Mack couldn't say.

"I'm glad she's safe, but we have to find out who this guy is."

"The cops will know that quickly, but so will we," Cal said, holding up a glass slide. "I accidentally got the guy to touch this." He gave her a wink. "I'll get Mina working on it back at Secure One. In the meantime, we have to assume that it's either tied to Dorian's reelection campaign or the body they found tonight."

"I'm leaning toward his reelection campaign," Mack said. "He's got enemies, and what better way to get you to back off something than to leverage the one person you love the most."

"Agreed," Cal said. "I think it was coincidence, or else the person behind the kidnapping got wind of the chaotic events tonight and decided he'd take advantage of it. It was smart to send someone in when there were already so many people in a tight space. You could get away without being noticed."

"Wait," Charlotte said, leaning forward. "The guy we got isn't the person behind the kidnapping?"

"Not according to him," Eric said, finally engaging with the team. "He told me he was hired to get the girl and bring her to a secure location where he'd hand her off for a big payday."

"More likely, he'd trade her for a bullet to the head," Cal muttered, and Eric pointed at him.

"So he was doing someone's dirty work. What does Senator Dorian think?" Selina asked while checking Charlotte's blood pressure.

Mack kept his gaze trained on the readout and was relieved when her blood pressure was normal.

"He thinks it has something to do with his future bid for the presidency," Eric said. "Mack's right. He's made enemies. There aren't many politicians who don't, but Dorian seems especially good at it. Someone saw an opportunity and took it tonight. I shouldn't have let you go alone to her room."

Charlotte brushed her free hand at him and sighed. "I

thought nothing of it either," she said, trying to reassure him. "When I took her up there, cops were everywhere. There was no way to know this guy would appear out of nowhere and attempt a kidnapping amid that much law enforcement."

"It was brazen," Cal said. "No doubt about it, but there's nothing we can do until Mina gets me a name and we can look into his past."

"I doubt it will lead us anywhere. I would bet my month's salary that he's got a laundry list of previous convictions and multiple addresses where he's lived," Eric said. It was easy to hear the frustration in his tone, which was mirrored in everyone's body language. It was after 3:00 a.m., and they'd been going for over eighteen hours. Everyone needed rest and food. Good thing their cook turned bodyguard had stocked the kitchen with easy-to-grab meals.

"Most likely," Cal agreed, "but you know Mina. All she needs is one tiny hint of a path, and she will find where it leads. We trust our team at home until we can get there, which won't be until tomorrow. Right now, we all need sleep." Heads nodded, and shoulders slumped at the idea of finally closing their eyes.

"Selina, let's keep Charlotte—"

A knock on the door interrupted Cal. "I want to talk to you, Newfellow!"

Mack heard Eric swear from the corner, giving him a mental fist bump. Dorian was the last person they needed to deal with right now.

"Let me do the talking," Cal said, and heads nodded as he opened the door to the senator and his entourage.

Dorian climbed the stairs and stood with his hands on

his hips in front of the team. "How in the hell did that happen?" he demanded, pointing behind him. "I pay you exorbitant amounts of money to keep the security tight on this place!"

Cal held up his hand and nodded. "You do, Senator. What happened tonight was unforgivable. I completely understand if you want to cancel your contract with Secure One. We let you down tonight."

Mack glanced at his boss with surprise and wasn't entirely sure that Cal didn't want exactly that to happen. Cal had grown tired of the senator's dramatics long before tonight. The man was fussy, ornery, demanding and never took the time to understand why or how something did or didn't work before he flew off the handle.

Ron Dorian's shoulders dropped an inch when he shook his head before he spoke. "I don't want to cancel my contract. I realize there were extenuating circumstances tonight that you had no control over. Though, I do want to know how that little thing in the corner was the only one around to save my daughter from a kidnapper!"

He gestured at Charlotte while he glared at the rest of the men in the room. Eric stood and walked toward the man. He wasn't going to follow Cal's no-talking order. "She was with your daughter because you put us in a room without access to necessary facilities. Ella is a sixteen-year-old girl who needed a restroom for reasons I don't think I should go into here. I sent the trained Secure One operative your daughter felt comfortable with and stayed in contact with them the entire time they were gone. I had all the exits covered, meaning no one was getting out of the house without an ID check." Eric held up his hand to the man who was ready to speak. "And before you ask, we don't know how he got inside. He may have snuck in when parents were coming and going with their kids. We will search our camera footage for that. When our operative indicated she needed help, I was there in less than twenty seconds to offer her assistance, though I'm sure it felt much longer to her and Ella. You can be unhappy with what happened here tonight, but our team did what we're trained to do regardless of the situation. So, yes, our trained operative in the corner currently nursing a concussion saved your daughter tonight, as any of us would have."

Eric faced off with the man for a moment and then stepped back and sat in the chair again. If a pin had dropped, everyone would have heard it. Mack couldn't remember the last time Eric had stepped up and taken the lead role. He wasn't sure he picked the right time to do it, but that was between him and Cal.

Dorian turned to Cal. "My daughter wants her," he said, pointing at Charlotte, "as her bodyguard until this guy is caught."

"Charlotte is not a bodyguard," Cal said.

"I don't care what you call her, but she will be by my daughter's side until this guy is behind bars."

"Sir—"

"Don't sir me," Dorian said. "Just listen. I want the girl, Mack, and the mouthy one," he pointed at Eric, "in my house in twenty minutes."

"I'll arrange it, sir," Cal said rather than continue to argue with him. "But Charlotte will need rest tonight. She can't take charge of your daughter until she is no longer concussed."

"That's what he is for," he said, pointing at Eric again.

"We both know she's in no shape to protect my daughter now, but Eleanor doesn't, so we'll let her continue to think Charlotte is her bodyguard while he provides the muscle. I want Mack there because I trust him to keep the perimeter safe."

"Eleanor is staying at the cabin and not returning to St. Paul?" Mack asked to clarify.

"I don't want my mother involved in this, so I'm keeping Ella here until they have the guy behind the kidnapping in handcuffs. She's on spring break this coming week, and if it takes longer than that to find the guy, she will do school online for the duration."

"I don't know how long I can be without two of my head men," Cal said, and Mack could hear in his voice that he was dead serious. Leaving Mack and Eric here meant a heavier workload at Secure One for the rest of the team. At least they wouldn't have to worry about Dorian's place, but that still spread them thin.

"Then you better find more guys or tell the police to hurry up. I have to fly to Washington for a vote. I will return to Minnesota once that is completed to prepare for my reelection campaign party. Understood?"

"Understood. I'll need to brief the team staying here and set them up with equipment in the morning. That means our mobile command will remain here until then."

"I'll need to assess Charlotte before we can leave as well," Selina added.

Mack bit back a smile. Everyone was tired of Dorian pushing them around, it appeared. He noticed that Charlotte had remained silent through the entire exchange. He glanced at her and noticed she was sagging in the chair. She needed rest.

"Dorian, I need a room for Charlotte immediately. She needs rest if she's going to hang out with Eleanor tomorrow," Mack said, taking a step forward.

"My staff has already readied a room. I'll see you there shortly."

Before anyone could respond, he turned and left the command center, his entourage closing in behind him and following him back to the house. When Mack turned back to the team, they were all awaiting Cal's orders.

"You heard the man. Mack, carry Charlotte to the house and get her settled."

"I can walk," she said, but Mack didn't like how soft her voice sounded. He glanced at Selina, who gave him a headshake. He'd be carrying her.

"Eric will follow you with bags for the night. Tomorrow, we'll regroup and figure this out. Nothing we can do until we've had some sleep."

Mack walked over to Charlotte and scooped her into his arms, her cry of surprise weak enough that everyone made way for them as he left the RV. Mack glanced down into the battered face of the woman in his arms and smiled.

"I know you feel like you went ten rounds with Mike Tyson, but remember, you were the hero we needed tonight. I'm so proud of you for not backing down and protecting Ella when she needed it."

"I've been Ella, and no one was there for me, Mack," she said as she rested her head against his chest. "I righted more than one wrong with a few of those kicks."

She fell quiet, and soon, her soft even breathing reached his ears. He wanted to rage against the world that she'd had to go through those things, but they had made her the strong determined woman who refused to shrink away from the flame. She had been burned so many times, but she proved to him tonight that she wasn't afraid to walk right back into the fire when it mattered most.

Her past made her a soldier.

What she'd done tonight made her a hero.

Chapter Six

The bus rumbled beneath her as she settled back into her seat and pulled a blanket up to her neck. The darkness surrounding the bus relaxed her. She was one step closer to safety. It had been sheer luck when she clicked on the radio in the truck and heard that news bulletin. Another woman had been found in the river, and she'd bet anything she'd once been in the same house in Pennsylvania. Her first piece of luck came when they mentioned a company, Secure One, had found her while working for a party at Senator Dorian's house outside of St. Paul.

When the sun came up, she ditched the truck and walked into a Salvation Army. They had bought her story that she was trying to return home to Minnesota but lost all her belongings and wallet when she accepted a ride with the wrong person. She had fought hard not to roll her eyes when she said it. She hadn't been given a choice when she took that ride, but she wasn't about to tell them that. They'd fed her, clothed her and bought her a bus ticket to St. Paul. Now all she had to do was figure out how to contact this Secure One place when she got there. She hoped they'd listen to her story and try to help her figure out this mess. Now that she knew The Miss was dead and The Madame was behind bars, she had to take the chance that Secure One could help her. If she didn't, she might as well have died in that room.

MACK TOOK IN the space around him. He was satisfied with the equipment Cal had given him to stay in touch with the team at Secure One. They'd be connected in real-time, and whenever they needed answers, someone would be there to give them. He didn't think Cal would stay gone long, but he did need to get back to Secure One and help Roman sort out their priorities before he returned to St. Paul. Mack was confident that he and Eric could handle any situation that arose. While they were in a holding pattern, he'd look for answers about the river deaths.

Before they left this morning, Selina checked Charlotte over one more time and gave her a list of things she should and shouldn't do with a concussion. Mack and Eric had plenty of experience taking care of head injuries and wouldn't let her do anything she shouldn't for a few days. When Charlotte woke this morning, she was chipper and not in much pain, so Selina was sure the bruises would stick around longer than the concussion. She was in the kitchen with Ella, making cookies and discussing art, which seemed to make Ella incredibly happy.

He hit the button on their quick connect link and waited while the system rang through to the Secure One control room.

"Secure one, Whiskey," a voice said.

"Secure two, Mike," he answered, and Mina's face popped up on the screen.

"Miss me already?" she asked with a chuckle.

"I didn't want you to think I didn't care." His wink made her smile. "I had a free minute and wanted to ask a favor."

"I'll do what I can."

"I know you have a database where you're keeping track of what rivers the women were found in, correct?"

"I cannot confirm nor deny that information."

Mack couldn't help but grin. She had been an FBI agent for years, and old habits died hard. The fact remained that she wasn't supposed to have that information and didn't get it through the proper channels at the FBI.

"Should you have that information, would you be able to highlight the rivers on a map for me? It would help me to see it laid out that way."

"If I have that information, I can send it through our secure channels in about an hour."

Mack pointed and winked. "Thanks, Min, you're the best."

"Are you hitting on my wife, sir?" Roman asked, sticking his face into the camera from behind Mina.

"Wouldn't dream of it," Mack answered with laughter. "I'm afraid of her husband."

"Someone should be since she's not. Are you guys managing okay over there? That was a hell of a night you had."

"We're good. It was a rough night, but it could have turned out worse than it did, so we'll take it as a win."

"How is our young scrappy one?" Mina asked. "I was terrified and proud all at the same time when Cal told us what she did."

Mack knew the feeling well. "I'm not sure if terrified even begins to cover it. I've been in combat situations that scared me less than the events of last night."

"It's okay, Mack," Roman said, leaning on the desk now. "It's okay to feel both of those things and admit you have a connection to her."

A brisk cross of his arms had Roman smirking before Mack even said a word. "A connection of commonality, maybe. Otherwise, that's a negative."

Roman and Mina had to bite back a snort, but Mina recovered first. "I'll prioritize that info and get it to you in a few minutes. Okay to tell Cal?"

"Of course," Mack agreed, straightening his back and letting go of the tension in his shoulders from their razzing. "I'm looking for a pattern, so if any of you find one, shout it out. We have to start somewhere."

Mina pointed at the camera. "Couldn't agree more. Whiskey, out."

The screen went blank, and Mack sighed as he lowered himself to a chair. They were right, there was a connection between him and Charlotte, but it was one he had to force himself not to think about or consider. They both had ghosts, but he wore his every day as a reminder that he had been weak when he should have been strong. He couldn't forgive himself for how those ghosts died, so there was no way she would ever look at him twice once she knew the truth. Being trapped here with her wasn't making it easier to distance himself, especially when he'd been the one to wake her every two hours last night.

The exhaustion wasn't helping him look at this case with a clear lens either. He forced his mind to look at the information analytically. What did they know about this guy? He pulled a pad of paper closer to him and grabbed a pen. In the beginning, he was impulsive but slowly, over time, perfected his presentation of his victims and his timeline. *Why didn't they find any victims for two years?* Mack underlined that question several times. Maybe he was in jail or out of the country? His last victim was found shortly before The Madame was arrested, and his next victim wasn't found until The Miss was in Arizona. *Coincidence?* Mack underlined that word several times too.

As far as they knew, the guy had to have connections to get the women and hold them somewhere. That is, assuming he'd held onto Layla for the whole of the eighteen months she'd been gone. Maybe he hadn't. Maybe he got her from someone else. Either way, he had to have connections and be cunning enough not to get caught. He would also need money and a vehicle. If he were using the same river repeatedly, it would be easy to pinpoint his location within the river's course, but he never used the same river twice.

He sat up immediately. That had been hiding in the back of his mind somewhere. He'd double-check when Mina sent him the map, but as far as he remembered, the women were never in the same river. Why was their perp driving around the country? Just to throw the feds off his tail? Was he getting the women from the same states, or was he transporting them already dead? Or was he transporting them alive and then killing them near the river?

Drawing a new column, he wrote the traits they knew the perp to have just by what his crimes revealed. He was connected, cunning, well-off, likely narcissistic, controlling and got off on having power over others. Mack paused with his pen on the pad. Maybe they were looking for this guy in all the wrong places. He dropped the pen and grabbed a laptop, then opened an incognito window. Narcissists like to talk about themselves. They yearned for accolades, even when they couldn't come right out and talk about their crimes.

Narcissists were everywhere, but Mack knew one place

a lot of them assembled to swap war stories, so to speak. There was a forum for everything, but some forums held darker content than others, and Mack intended to start his search there.

Chapter Seven

Mack stood in the makeshift office and stared at the map projected on the wall. Something was bugging him about this case, but he couldn't put his finger on it.

"Mack?" a voice asked from the doorway, and he turned to see Charlotte peeking in the door. "Everything okay? It's late."

"Everything's fine," he said. "It is late. Why are you still up?"

Her smile brightened his day no matter when she hit him with it, and tonight was no different. Her black eye and bruised chin didn't detract from her beauty. In fact, in his eyes, those bruises reminded him that behind her beauty was an irrefutable strength few people had.

She stepped into the room and walked past the large wooden desk the senator used when he was home. Now it held Secure One computers and link-ups to headquarters. They had a dead body and attempted kidnapping on their watch, and he wasn't any happier about it than Cal. While it was beyond their control, it also put their name back in the media. Cal had tried to minimize publicity about their security service since The Miss was killed, but it appeared the universe was not cooperating with him.

"That or this is still tied to The Madame," Mack muttered.

"What now?" Charlotte asked, her back stiffening at the utterance of her former boss's name.

"I'm sorry." He grimaced at himself. "I didn't mean to say that aloud. I was thinking about how we can't keep Secure One out of the news no matter how hard we try. Cal is frustrated that The Madame and The Miss have kept us on the public's radar."

"And you think all of this," she motioned around the map, "is tied to The Madame?"

"I don't know, but according to Roman and Mina, several women were found in rivers while The Madame was operating." His head swung back and forth in frustration as he tried to see a pattern that wasn't there.

"What is this?" Charlotte pointed at the map of the United States. "Rivers?"

"Yeah," he said, his hand going through his short brown hair in frustration. Unlike Cal, he'd gotten rid of the high and tight hairstyle the moment he left the field on a stretcher. His boss liked to tease him that he looked like an FBI agent now, just like Roman. He'd shake his head in disdain but be laughing while he did it. "Each highlighted river represents a place where at least one body was found since they started finding women. The most recent women were wearing red gowns."

"So, the bodies found in the rivers while The Madame was in operation weren't in red?" she asked.

"Not according to Mina. It was only when the recent bodies were discovered that they were wearing red gowns. A news reporter dubbed him The Red River Slayer, and it stuck." The moniker might be accurate, but something about it set his teeth on edge.

"If you think about it, I could have been one of those women."

Mack sucked in air through his nose. "I try not to think about that, okay?"

"I think about it all the time." She stared at the wall rather than make eye contact with him. "When they found the first woman, I was new to the Red Rye House. When other women I lived with started disappearing, I thought they left of their own free will. But I was naive enough back then to believe we could leave."

"But you didn't know if the women who disappeared were the women they found."

Her shrug gave him the answer. "How could I? It wasn't like we were allowed to watch or listen to the news. We were very sheltered in Red Rye."

"Nothing?" Mack asked in surprise with a lifted brow.

"Nothing. We had no cable or news channels on the television, and all we could do was stream movies. We also didn't have a radio. I heard about them finding the women on the radio when I was on a *date*," which she put in quotation marks, "but they said they hadn't identified them yet. Not that they *couldn't* identify them. I didn't find that out until I left The Miss and came here."

"And now we've found another woman from The Miss."

"Layla." She said the name with reverence. As though saying it that way gave her an identity. "When she disappeared, I figured The Miss sold or killed her. She wasn't bringing any money in, and The Miss didn't put up with that for long."

"And she disappeared eighteen months ago?" Mack asked again.

"I thought about it, and the timeline is correct within a few months. I've already been at Secure One for six months, and she disappeared about a year before I surrendered."

"This is the first time we've had a timeline. You're the reason we have it, even if you did disobey orders. We'll have to talk about your propensity to do that."

"Last time I checked, Cal's my boss, not you." She looked him up and down in a way that brought a smile to his lips.

"Noted, but when you're here with me, I'm the boss regarding quick decisions as the situation warrants."

"Accepted, but I will protect Ella no matter the cost. You may as well know that."

"I do," he promised, tracing his thumb over her jaw, the bump smaller after a night of rest and ice. "But I don't have to like it. Have you always been this brave, Char?"

Her blue eyes held his, and he watched her wrap her arms around herself in a hug. "No. I used to live in fear every second of the day. I was afraid of my foster parents and siblings when I was a kid. When I hit the streets, I was afraid of the dark and the things it held, so I painted at night. It was safer to be awake and see them coming. When I started working for The Madame, I was afraid of the men she made me date. When I started working for The Miss, I was afraid of everything."

"What changed?"

"Me." Her answer was simple, but he knew the explanation was far more complicated. "When I looked back on my life, fear was the common thread running through it. I could keep being afraid and keep being taken advantage of, or I could snip the thread of fear and see what happened."

Mack nodded, the explanation making sense to him. "I understand." Her snort was sarcastic and pithy. He turned her chin to meet his gaze. "I know you don't think so, but I do. My dad and I were in a car accident when I was a toddler. I lived. He didn't. My mother struggled the rest of her life with the fear of losing me. She didn't let me do anything out of fear that I'd get hurt and die too. I grew up thinking every new experience was scary and should be avoided. Our experiences were different, there is no doubt, but I understand what you mean by a thread of fear. I had to cut mine too."

"When you went into the service?"

"No, when my mother got cancer when I was a teenager, I realized she wasn't going to make it. Suddenly, I had to figure out how to live unafraid."

"I'm still afraid a lot of the time, but I tell myself that when I do something even while I'm afraid, the next thing I have to do will be a little easier."

A smile lifted his lips, and he nodded. "You're right, and it's working. I remember the woman who surrendered to us six months ago, and she's not the same woman standing before me today."

This time, it was her smile that beamed back at him. "I'm glad someone noticed. I've worked hard in therapy to accept that a lot of what's happened to me was done to me and not something I did to myself."

"That's important to remember," Mack agreed. It was true for her, but not for him. What happened to him was something he had done to himself. He only had to look at his boots to be reminded of that.

"I argued that I did make a lot of bad choices, and the therapist agreed, but she also pointed out that I never had any good choices to start with."

"She makes a point."

Charlotte tipped her head in agreement and crossed her arms over her chest. "After I thought about it, I decided that I could continue to make bad choices or start from scratch and make better ones. Go to therapy. Work a job. Be part of a team instead of going it alone."

"The changes you've made the last six months haven't been overlooked. I hope you know that. We're all incredibly proud of you."

Mack noted the pink creep up her cheeks at his compliment. That was something else she needed to learn how to accept—how integral she was to the team.

"Thank you," she said, glancing down at the floor.

He tipped her chin up again and held her gaze. "Hold your head high, Charlotte. You've got grit and proved it, including when you fought off someone twice your size to protect a young girl. That takes guts. How is your head?"

"Okay," she said with a shy smile. "I'm being careful and following Selina's orders so I don't make anything worse. It's been fun hanging out and being with Ella today, but I'm ready to work now."

"Eric is here to protect Ella."

"Understood, but I can help in other ways. Let me help you figure this out." She motioned at the map and took a step closer. "Some of these rivers run through more than one state. How do we know what location he put them in the river?"

"We don't," Mack answered with frustration. "That's part of the problem. Obviously, everything floats downstream, and some rivers run through several states. For instance, the Mississippi flows through seven states. It's nearly impossible to know where the body was dumped."

"Which means he gets away with it longer because these rivers run all over the country. Well, except for Layla."

Mack's attention shifted from the map to the woman who always, despite her ordeal, had a ready smile. Her long blond hair was wavy, and she wore it tied behind her head with a band. Her blue eyes were luminous in the light from the projector, even with a black eye, and her lips were pursed as she finished the last word.

"Except for Layla?"

"Think about it, Mack," she said, stepping in front of him to point at the map. Her body slid across his in a whisper of material that sent a burning need straight through him. "She was found outside St. Paul, right?" He nodded, and she raised her hand to point at the top of the map. "And we know the Mississippi originates at Lake Itasca. That's what, about three hours north of where she was found?"

How had he not thought of that? She was right. The Mississippi headwaters were only an hour from Secure One, the way the crow flies.

"We should have thought of that," he said, snapping the projector off and leaving the lights low. "Thank you for pointing it out. I can't believe we missed something so obvious."

Her tiny hand waved his words away. "The difference is that you have too much information about all the other women. Since I don't know anything about those cases, my mind tracked the possibilities for just Layla. Do you think that means the killer is from Minnesota?"

Mack didn't cut himself any slack despite her insistence. He should have been concentrating on one woman's journey at a time instead of as a group. That was exactly what he would do tomorrow. He'd focus solely on each woman and see if a pattern developed rather than as a whole, where the pattern seemed willy-nilly.

"There's no way to know that, but my gut says no. The women have been found in rivers all over the country. In the beginning, the bodies were found randomly, then we had a period of inactivity, and now, they're finding a woman every six weeks."

"Which means we only have about five weeks until another woman like Layla is found," Charlotte said, and Mack noticed a shiver go up her spine.

He didn't stop himself from reaching over to tenderly rub the base of her back. "I'm sorry. You shouldn't have to keep witnessing women you know dying in this way."

"Those women didn't do anything to deserve this. They were looking for a better life than one on the streets, just like I was, so as long as I'm still breathing, I'll fight for them."

"I know," Mack assured her, pulling her into him and wrapping his arm around her shoulder. "We know the women were innocent victims. The FBI has known that for years, but when the perp was killing women with no identities, they had nothing to go on."

"They never convinced The Madame or her husband to tell them who the women were?"

Mack wished he could hide his anger when he shook his head, but he knew she could see the way his jaw pulsed at the idea of how badly the FBI had botched the investigation. "Of course not. If they admitted they knew who the women were, it would implicate them in their murders. I'm sure their lawyers told them to remain silent."

"True," she agreed. "Do you have a list of the victims along with when and where they were found?"

"Yes."

"Good, then we take it one step further and mark the exact location where a body was found on the map."

"That still doesn't tell us where the body was dumped."

He felt her shrug under his hand before she spoke. "Just trying to help."

Mack swore internally for shooting her down. "I'm sorry," he said, turning her to face him. "I'm frustrated with this case. It's hard when I know that every time the sun comes up, another woman is one day closer to death. I may no longer be in the army, but I'll always be someone who wades into battle to save the innocents. This," he said with frustration as he flicked his hand at the projector, "has to stop."

Char braced her delicate hand on his chest, and her warmth spread through him like wildfire. It calmed and centered him. She made such a difference in his life just by being in it, and she grounded him when he was ready to pop off into the atmosphere from frustration. She was also the calming touch he needed when he wanted to rage against the world, and he wasn't sure how he felt about that. He could never be with this woman, so having that kind of reaction to her was problematic.

"If anyone can find this guy, Secure One can. You work together to save the people you care about, and that's what makes the team successful. Maybe a pattern will naturally develop if you plot out the places where the women were found."

Mack ran a hand down his face as he stared at the map. "You're right. I'll have Mina do it tomorrow since she has the kind of mind that will see the pattern developing as she goes."

"She'll also be rested, and you're not, Mack. You need to sleep, or you won't be any good to anyone."

He shut off the computer and walked with her to the door. "I'll try to sleep, but I'll end up staring at the ceiling until the sun comes up."

Her laughter was genuine when it reached his ears. "Some nights, I'd rather stare at the ceiling than deal with the nightmares."

"Those are the nights I find you in the kitchen," Mack pointed out as he shut the lights off.

"There's something comforting about a quiet kitchen at two a.m. with the scent of bread baking in the oven. I'd rather be tired and busy than tired and idle."

"It leaves too much time to think," they said in unison.

She glanced at him for a moment with a look of consideration, sympathy and understanding in her blue eyes before she waved and turned away from him. He stood rooted in place until she disappeared. As he walked to his room, the memories of his time with Char filled him. She was far more intuitive than she understood, which made him wonder why she was the way she was. Life on the street hardened a person, but something happened to her before she found herself on the street. What was it? That was the question. Mack was sure the answer would be no more forthcoming than his answer to the question she'd asked one night in the kitchen.

What happened out there in that giant sandbox no one wants to play in, Mack?

There were things he wouldn't discuss with anyone, and that included Charlotte. One of those things was the sandbox that held nothing but pain and regret. Charlotte had enough of those two things in her short life.

Chapter Eight

Charlotte didn't want to wait for Mina to plot the rivers that once held women in their watery grip. She didn't work well with computer-generated models, so she'd drawn her own map of the United States and marked the rivers in their full routes through each state, including their tributaries. Now all she needed were the locations of the bodies. That was easy enough to find. She brought up Google and typed in *The Red River Slayer victims*; within three seconds, she had the list she needed. She plotted the city or town closest to where the victim was brought ashore. That would only help them if they needed information from local authorities.

There was a knock on the office door, and Charlotte glanced up, expecting Mack or Eric, but Ella stood there instead. "Hey," she said to the girl. "Did you need something?"

"Not really. I'm bored, and Eric is hovering. He can go grab some food if I'm in here with you."

Charlotte motioned her in and then closed the office door and locked it. Eric and Mack had a key, but no one else did. "I can't say I'm not boring, but you're welcome to hang out here."

"What are you working on?" Ella asked, taking in the

map. "This is huge. How did you find paper big enough for a map?"

"It's parchment paper from the kitchen."

"Really?" She was surprised when she ran her hand over it and realized it was true. "I never thought about drawing on it."

"I like it for certain projects, especially when heavy markers are involved because it doesn't bleed through the back."

Ella's finger followed the rivers on the map with her head cocked. "Rivers? What are the numbers and the towns?" Charlotte didn't have a chance to say anything before Ella let out a shocked breath. "The women from The Red River Slayer?"

"You shouldn't see this," Charlotte said, starting to roll it up, but Ella slapped her hand down on it.

"Please, I'm practically an adult, and it's not like any of this is a huge secret. The last woman was found just steps outside this door."

"I just don't want to get in trouble with the senator. I'm supposed to guard you, not get you involved in a murder case."

Ella brushed her words away with her hand. "He's not here, and trust me when I say he has no idea what I'm doing most of the time." She fell silent and tapped her chin, repeatedly pointing at the rivers as though she were counting. She opened her phone, grabbed the blue marker, and made lines in several states. After more pecking on her phone, she grabbed a red one and made similar lines in others.

"What are you doing?"

"He's hit the Mississippi, Kansas, Arkansas, Red, Rio Grande, Chattahoochee, Missouri, Platte, Snake, Colorado, Canadian and Tennessee rivers, which run through both predominately blue and red states."

"You're talking about politics?" Charlotte asked, and Ella nodded. "I don't follow politics."

"I was thinking about it when they found the woman here. My dad is running for reelection, so I wondered if politics were the reason for the murders. If you look at the map, the blue or red line means a senator from that party is running for reelection this year. The color of the line indicates a democrat or republican."

"Seriously?"

"I mean, yeah, I know this stuff because of my dad."

"Are these all the senators running for reelection?"

"Oh, no, there are more. We'd have to make the map a little more detailed, but then I could tell you who was running in what state."

Charlotte grabbed the black marker and finished drawing the state lines until she had a complete map of the forty-eight states. She stepped aside and let Ella finish marking the map with senators running for reelection. When they finished, they stared at the map while Charlotte did some fast math in her head. "There are a lot of states that still haven't been touched."

"For sure," Ella agreed. "Every two years, a third of the Senate is up for reelection. This year there are thirty-three."

Charlotte tipped her head to the side. "But wait. Some of these murders occurred more than two years ago." She put an *X* next to the ones found when the murders started. There were six of those women.

Ella shrugged as though she'd grown bored with the whole thing. "I'm probably wrong, but at least you have the information on the map now." Her phone rang, and she looked at the caller ID before she hit the decline button. "That was my grandma. I'm going to go up to my room and call her back. She wants to FaceTime to prove I'm still alive." Her eye roll was heavy, as was her sigh.

Charlotte grabbed a walkie off the table. "Secure two, Charlotte."

"Secure one, Echo," Eric replied, which he wouldn't do if he were being forced, and then the key slid into the lock and the door opened.

"Ella is ready to return to her room," Charlotte said, patting her shoulder. "Thanks, Eric."

"No problem. The place is quiet. I'll take her up and stay with her. Mack is grabbing a bite, and then he'll be in."

Charlotte nodded and waved as Ella left. Her mind should be on the case, but instead, she was busy picturing the dark brown eyes of the man in the kitchen. The man who starred in her dreams, both day and night. It was becoming a problem, and she didn't know how to fix it.

WHEN MACK WALKED into the office, Charlotte was pacing and muttering to herself. He stood by the door and watched her for longer than he should, but he was taken by her strength and determination to be part of this team. She could do her job and go back to her room, but she didn't do that. She jumped in with both feet and worked the problem with them until it was resolved. Usually, her role was to bring them dinner in the boardroom or command center because they couldn't leave the monitors, but she always stayed. She stayed and offered suggestions from a different perspective they didn't have. That of a woman who had been attacked more times than Mack cared to think about and as a woman kept as property somewhere that looked completely normal. Charlotte always added to the conversation, which was why he wasn't surprised she was trying to work the problem now.

"Charlotte?" he asked from the doorway, and she jumped, spinning to stare at him with her hand on her chest.

"You scared me."

"Sorry," he said, pushing off the door and walking to her. He rubbed her arms gently and waited for her to settle again. "You were so lost in thought you didn't notice me come in. What has you so worked up?" Her gaze darted to the side, and that was when he noticed the map on the table.

His hands fell from her arms, and he walked over to the table to take in the map. "What's this?"

"It's nothing," she said quickly, attempting to roll it up. Mack held it down.

"It's obviously something. These are rivers in the United States. What are the other symbols?"

Charlotte brought him up to speed on the plotted areas and the colored markings. His mouth was hanging open by the time she finished. She must have noticed because she held up her hand to him as though he shouldn't speak.

"I can't make it work either. There was a two-year pause on the murders, but his original victims were before this election cycle."

That break from the murders would haunt them and keep them from solving this case. Mack was sure of it.

Two years.

"Senators run for reelection every two years," Mack said, thinking out loud.

"Yes," Charlotte agreed. "Ella said that every two years, a third of the Senate is up for reelection."

"Okay, so six women died three years ago, which would have been during the previous reelection cycle. You might be onto something here," Mack said in disbelief. "I need to call Mina." He sat and fired up their connection to Secure One. Once they were hooked up, he pulled the tablet from its moorings and walked around the table. He wanted to show Mina the extensive map Charlotte had drawn.

"Secure two, Whiskey." Mina's voice was heard over the tablet, but there was no video.

"Secure one, Mike," Mack answered, and Mina's face popped up on the screen.

"Miss me already?"

Mack noted the smile on Charlotte's face from the corner of his eye before speaking. "I always miss you, Mina, but this time I have a question."

"What do you mean, this time? You always have a question."

Charlotte snorted while trying to hold in her laughter, and Mack chuckled. "Fair point. This one is about our perp. First, I want you to check out this map."

Mack held the tablet out and scanned the extensive map while he filled her in on their theory that the killings may be politically driven.

"That's an interesting theory," Mina said, her head tipped. "What is your question?"

"You were around when the original women were found, correct?"

"Yes," she answered immediately. "Well, for some of them. Others were found while I was on the run, but since it made national news, I was aware of them."

"Then my question is do the early murders mirror our current ones?"

Mina blinked several times before she spoke. "Do you mean in their cause of death?"

"Cause of death and the way they're dressed. That kind of thing."

"Oh, no," she said immediately.

"The new murders differ from the original murders two years ago?" Charlotte asked with surprise.

"Well, the cause of death has been consistent. Always strangulation. From what I read in the FBI documents, the first six women had obvious strangulation marks on their necks. Those were the bodies found during The Madame's time in Red Rye."

"The new victims do not," Mack pointed out immediately.

"No, they don't, but they had broken hyoid bones, which only happens when someone is strangulated."

"What's a hyoid bone?" Charlotte asked.

Mack glanced at her and noted her deep concentration. She wanted to understand, so he nodded at Mina to answer.

"Your hyoid bone looks like a horseshoe, and it's under your chin here," Mina said, lifting her head to point at the spot at the top of her trachea. "Essentially, it connects the tongue and voice box and supports the airway. When it breaks—"

"The airway collapses, and you can't breathe," Charlotte finished.

Mina pointed at her. "Smart girl, and that's correct. Of course, if the bone is fractured in a different setting, the person often survives after seeking treatment. However, in strangulation cases, normally, the bone isn't just fractured but obliterated. Therefore, the victim dies from lack of airway."

Charlotte ran her hand under her chin near her neck. "Isn't strangulation usually lower though? Like here?" She motioned at her mid-trachea while Mina nodded.

"That is where the six original women had strangulation marks."

"What about the presentation of the victims?"

"Negative," Mina replied. "The first six women were dumped. Some were naked. Others were just in their underclothes."

"Are we dealing with two different perps?" Mack asked with frustration.

"Not necessarily. It's not uncommon for serial killers to perfect their game. At the FBI, we called it developing a method. They often start killing helter-skelter—"

"Coined by another serial killer," Mack said grimly.

"The difference is Charles Manson was a psychopath who never killed anyone. He convinced other people to do it for him. That's not the case with our perp."

"You're saying that maybe during the period he wasn't killing women, he was learning and improving his technique?"

"We can't say he didn't kill women during that time. We just didn't find any."

"Fair point," Mack agreed. "Assuming it's the same guy, he's figured out how to strangle without leaving marks and decides to present the women rather than just toss them?"

"Strangulation is generally a crime of passion. Where

the hyoid bone sits, the victim would have to be lying down for him to break it without leaving ligature marks."

"Like during sex."

"That's exactly right. Or, at the very least, he must be the one with leverage and power."

Mack briefly slid his eyes to Charlotte and then back to the tablet. "That was helpful, thanks. Should we proceed with the assumption that this is the same guy?"

"That or it's a copycat with better techniques."

"What is your gut telling you, Mina?" Mack asked her point-blank because he needed to know if he should pivot on this investigation.

"My gut says it's the same guy. He craves power. He may have a job where he has no power or he may have a job where he has all the power. That's not exactly helpful, unless you consider that he keeps these women for long periods and drives around the country to dump them in different rivers."

"That would lead a person to believe he has a job with power and money," Charlotte said from behind him.

Mina pointed at her from the camera. "Exactly. Our perp likely has a powerful job but one that doesn't fulfill him the way controlling a woman does. Having power over a woman he can force to bend to his every whim turns him on. Strangulation is always a crime of passion in this kind of setting. It's possible he has certain kinks that lend themselves to strangulation or he could kill them accidentally when he loses control. I suspect the first few times that was the case. He killed them by accident, so he dumped the bodies just to get rid of them. The next few times were intentional, but he still hadn't perfected his technique. What happened over the next two years,

I don't know, but I still believe it's the same person killing these women now. I'm not sold on it being politically driven though."

"It's just a working theory," Charlotte jumped in. "I thought it was a good train of thought to follow for now."

"Agreed—"

The walkie-talkie buzzed to life, and Charlotte grabbed it. "Secure One? This is the estate security guard at the gate. I need assistance."

Charlotte pushed the button so Mack could speak. "Assistance? Is there a threat?"

"I don't think she's a threat, but she's demanding to talk to someone from Secure One. The person who killed The Miss is what she said."

"The Miss?" Charlotte asked, her gaze traveling to Mina's, who sat frozen on the screen while she listened to the exchange.

She released the button, and another voice filled the room. "Charlotte! Oh, my God, Charlotte, is that you?"

Within one second, Mack noticed Mina's and Charlotte's eyes widen when they heard the voice. Charlotte did nothing but hold the walkie with her mouth hanging open, so Mack grabbed it and depressed the button. "We'll be right down."

"I know that voice, so I'll inform the team that the game just changed," Mina said, her voice tight. "Call me back as soon as you have a handle on this."

"Ten-four. Mike, out."

Chapter Nine

"Charlotte." Mack was in front of her, taking hold of her shaking hands. "Charlotte, you need to breathe. Breathe in and then out," he said, demonstrating until she did the same thing. His warm hand grasped her chin. "You look like you've seen a ghost."

"I heard one," she whispered, shaking her head to clear it. "I think that was Bethany."

"Bethany?"

Her exaggerated nod continued until he gently grasped her chin to stop it. "She was one of the women who disappeared when she challenged The Miss."

The light came on in his eyes, and he took a small breath. "Bethany and Emelia."

"It's been almost two years. I thought for sure they were dead."

He grabbed her hand and started pulling her behind him. "Let's head to the gate and check this out. I need to let Eric know to stay put."

He brought the walkie to his lips to contact Eric, but Charlotte's mind was on the woman at the gate. If she had been alive all this time, where had she been? Why didn't she come back when she learned The Miss was dead? Was she alone, or was Emelia with her? Lost in thought, she didn't notice Mack stop until she ran up against him, her body plastered against the length of his back. He was hot in every way a man could be, and her skin tingled from the contact she worked so hard to avoid.

She was still daydreaming about how warm he was when he held her out by the shoulder. "Charlotte, where's your head?"

"My head?"

"We can't go out there if your head is not in the game. This could be a trick. They could be trying to lure us out to leave Eric vulnerable or take us out. I want you to stay behind me at all times."

"But Bethany," she whispered, her voice breaking on the name.

"If Bethany is out there and alone, we'll make a new plan. We have to proceed with caution until we know otherwise. Okay?"

After taking a breath in and letting it out, Charlotte nodded. "I'm good. It threw me to hear her voice again, but you're right, it could be a trick." She patted the gun at the small of her back. The one they insisted she carry after the last kidnapping attempt on Ella. "I still have my gun from when I was alone with Ella earlier."

"Good, be ready to use it. Just make sure none of us are in the line of fire."

They had a short walk to the front door, but the walk to the front gate was a couple of hundred feet. The cabin was gated, but that didn't mean someone couldn't approach by water and sneak onto the property from the river with no one the wiser. They both pulled their guns, and started their walk, their heads on a swivel. They made it to the gate without difficulty. The night guardsman stood inside the booth while a blond woman sat on a stool across from him.

"Oh, my God, it's her," she whispered to Mack. They waited until the guard opened the gate for them to approach the booth. "Bethany?"

The woman glanced up, and instantly, her face crumpled. "Charlotte! It is you. I heard your voice, but I couldn't believe it." She never said another word, just cried silent tears, her body spasming from the emotion.

"Is she alone?" Mack asked Lucas, the guard.

"As far as I can tell."

"Is this a trick, Bethany?" Charlotte asked the woman. She had lost weight and was paler than anyone she'd ever seen before.

"No, not a trick," the woman answered. "I need help. I heard on the news that another woman was found by the people who killed The Miss. I didn't know where else to go. I'm—I'm in danger." Her last sentence was whispered with so much fear that Charlotte's gut clenched from reflex. She knew that kind of fear.

Charlotte glanced at Mack and waited for him to make a decision. He lifted a brow and then tipped his head before he spoke. "We'll take her from here, Lucas," he told the guard. "Be on high alert just in case this is an attack we don't see coming."

"It's not," Bethany said in a choked whisper. "I've been on a bus and came straight here. I haven't spoken to anyone and no one knows who I am. I swear."

Mack made a hand signal that Charlotte recognized as the two and one formation. She was to walk with Bethany into the house while he brought up the rear. It was her job to police their approach. Her hand was shaking when she switched her gun to her right hand and motioned Bethany out of the security hut. The woman ran to her and threw her arms around Charlotte, nearly knocking them both to the ground if it hadn't been for Mack grabbing her belt loop at the back of her pants. His warmth there helped ground her as the woman in her arms sobbed incoherently.

"We have to move," Mack said in her ear, sending a shiver down her spine both from desire and fear.

After a nod, she convinced Bethany to walk to the house, but she couldn't help but think Mina was correct and the game had changed. Her biggest fear was that The Miss hadn't stayed buried after all.

WHEN MACK WALKED back into the office, Charlotte was hunched over her pad, the swish of her charcoal pencil the only sound in the room. He wasn't sure if she was breathing as she concentrated on the pad.

"Is Bethany settled?"

The jolt of her body told him she hadn't known he was there. Her pencil fell to the desk, and she quickly closed the sketch pad and rested her elbow on it.

"Sorry, I didn't hear you come in. She's resting in the room next to Ella. I helped her shower, and she had something to eat. Now we wait."

"Do you think she needs more medical care than Selina can provide?"

Cal, Selina, Roman and Mina were in the chopper, and they'd arrive within the hour. Charlotte was glad because they needed more help than they had, but understandably, Cal didn't want to involve the police just yet.

"She's thin, but overall, physically healthy. I think she will need a lot of mental health care after what happened.

I don't even know where she's been the last two years, but it was nowhere good."

"I agree, which is why I'm glad Cal is coming in. We need to ask the right questions, and Mina is excellent at that. Once Bethany can give us some answers, we'll let Selina decide what kind of care she needs and where."

"I want to know where Emelia is, Mack. Those two were inseparable."

"She may not know, so don't get too hung up on the need for one answer, Char. This could be as simple as she was hiding from The Miss and didn't know she was dead until now."

Charlotte raised her brow at him slowly. "If she had been hiding out, she would have heard The Miss was dead, Mack. I suspect wherever she was living, it wasn't by choice. My guess would be she's been a captive woman the last two years."

Mack's jaw set and pulsed once as an answer. "The tentacles of those two women always seem to work themselves back into our lives. One's in prison, and one's dead, but we still aren't free of them."

"And never will be, Mack," she whispered, staring at her feet. "Ever."

He pulled her into his arms just as a shudder went through her. He cursed himself for not thinking before he spoke. "I'm sorry, that was insensitive," he whispered. "I'm frustrated, but I often forget those women ruined your life, not mine."

"Not true," she countered, stepping out of his arms. "You carry the burden of killing The Miss."

"I carry no burden about her death, Char. Sometimes

the right choice is to take a life if it prevents them from hurting others. I learned that first hand in the army."

He walked toward her. Her blue globes filled with fear, and he paused, holding his next step. Was she afraid of him? "You don't need to be afraid of me, Charlotte."

"I—I'm not," she stuttered before she pushed the pad behind her from where she rested on the edge of the desk.

"I see the look in your eyes when I move toward you too quickly. I try to give you your space because I know that feeling inside your chest when terror grips your heart," he whispered, holding his hand near his chest. "It's all you can do to stop yourself from running."

"I'm not afraid of you, Mack. I just know it's smart to keep you at arm's length. I don't trust easily, but I trust you. That scares me more than anything."

Mack cocked his head. "Because trusting me means I could hurt you?" Her head barely tipped in acknowledgment. "I wouldn't do that, Charlotte. I've been where you're at." He held up his hand to stem her words. "I mean that I've been traumatized, hurt and let down by the people who were supposed to look out for me. The feeling of betrayal is so powerful you can taste it. That's when you realize the only person you can trust is yourself. Am I close?"

"Spot on," she agreed in a whispered tone. "Looking back, I can see that has been true since day one. It took me too long to see it, and the one time I tried to take care of myself, I ended up a pawn in someone else's game. I don't want to be that again."

"You aren't." Mack took another step until he was right in front of her, staring down into her tired blue eyes. He expected her to cower at an entire foot taller than her, but she didn't. She held her ground and lifted her chin. "At Secure One, you're an equal team member."

"I'm the cook. I don't think that's equal to anyone, Mack. That's the hired help."

He laid his finger against her lips. "Wrong. That's not how Cal runs Secure One, and you know it. Everyone contributes to the success of the business. As the cook, you're one of the most important people on the team. We're a group of big guys with healthy appetites, but we can't tell a saucepan from a broiler. You fuel us, which is one less thing we have to worry about when we're busy. It may feel like you're in the background, but you're not. Never doubt that."

Her nod was quick as his gaze traveled to the pad behind her. "You've also contributed to the team with your art. Cal took your suggestions to the client and secured the job as their security company because of your work. He'll square up with you for your contributions. Talent is talent, Charlotte, regardless of our pasts, abilities or disabilities. We aren't one-dimensional."

"I know," she said, sliding her hand up his chest to rest there.

It was as though she knew the secrets that he held but couldn't say.

He allowed himself the pleasure of grasping her tiny hand in his for a moment before he pulled her into a hug when her eyes said yes. With one arm, he held her, and with the other, he flipped the lid open on her sketch pad. When she hid what she was working on, he knew it was important to her. He took in the image on the pad and froze. The next breath wouldn't come as he stared at himself dressed in army fatigues. He was looking over his shoulder with sheer terror on his face. His gaze traveled down the pad to see his pants in tattered, jagged edges at the knees. He wore no boots or socks but had open wounds and blood pooling around his feet that congealed into a broken heart. It was the blood falling from the wounds on the left that broke him.

Has been. Useless. Inadequate. Failure.

The right leg told a different story.

Hope. Victory. Skill. Knowledge. New life.

When his lungs finally released a breath, it sounded like a grunt of pain. He stumbled backward until he hit the wall. "How did you know?"

Charlotte glanced at him in confusion and then at the pad. Her grimace was noticeable when she turned back to him. "I didn't want you to see that."

"Then why did you draw it?"

"I draw what I see, Mack. I'm an artist. It's how I express emotion."

"I don't understand how you knew about my legs."

"I see more than you think," she answered. "I noticed when you were changing your boots and socks that night in the mobile command unit, but I also saw the metal bars across your boots and how your gait is slightly different than the other guys. I asked Roman about it, and all he would say was you were injured in a mission gone wrong. He said the injury was the reason why you left the army."

A mission gone wrong. More like a mission that blew up in his face. Literally.

Chapter Ten

Mack rubbed his hands over his face while he paced the room. She was silent, but he worried it was in judgment rather than patience. "I don't talk about this with anyone, Charlotte."

"I'm not asking you to, Mack. My drawings are for me. They help me process the emotions that are too big to hold inside. I don't know how you were hurt or why. Chances are, what I drew is all wrong, but that's what I see."

The nod of his head was barely there, and she fell silent, staring at her hands rather than meeting his gaze. "We were moving a diplomat and his family to a safe house."

"You don't have to tell me, Mack," she said, halting his words. "That's not why I drew it."

He lifted his chin to hold her gaze. Her blue eyes didn't hold pity as he'd expected. They were open and clear, their depths holding some of the same pain and experiences in his. They'd both fought battles that hadn't ended up in the win column.

"Maybe I don't have to tell you," he said, not breaking eye contact, "but that drawing…" He shook his head and dropped his gaze to the floor. "It brought everything back. Without knowing it, you captured my emotions, from my expression to the words that bled from my soul. Maybe I have to tell someone, so I can finally be free of the shame."

"You have nothing to be ashamed of, Mack."

"You don't know that," he whispered. "The truth is I ran the wrong way. I protected the wrong team."

"I don't believe that." Her refusal was punctuated with her arms crossing over her chest in defiance.

"My job was to protect the diplomat, and I failed to do that, Charlotte. The caravan made it to the safe house without attracting any attention from the insurgents. I was driving the diplomat and his family while my team sandwiched us. The front half of the team was securing the area for me. I told the diplomat, his family and the traveling security team to wait while I reconned with Cal. I climbed from the car and walked toward him when I heard the back door of the car squeak open. That was the last sound I heard before an explosion rocked the air. I glanced behind me to see the fireball from the diplomat's car. I didn't run back, Charlotte. I ran toward Cal and the team like a coward!"

"Mack, no," she said, her tone soft and nonjudgmental. "What made you run for the team?"

He tossed his hand up, the smell of fire and fuel stuck in his head as he relived those moments. "The car was nothing more than a burning shell instantly, but we're trained to render aid, and I didn't."

"If nothing was left but a burning shell, is it safe to say that you knew with just one look that everyone in that car was already gone?"

"Without a doubt." The breath he let out was heavy and filled with disappointment. Disappointment in himself.

"I still should have gone back. Instead, I ran toward my team, worried they'd been hit by flying debris."

"When the truth was, you had been."

His nod was immediate and short. "I was screaming for them to get down and find cover, but they ran toward me. Cal and Roman caught me as I fell, dragged me into a vehicle and took off. I don't remember anything else until I woke up in the hospital."

"And what did you learn when you woke up?"

He stood and paced to the window, pulling the curtain back a hair to stare into the darkness. "They think the bomb was set to detonate when the back door opened. I'm sure whoever rigged it never thought we'd get past loading them into the vehicle. It was just chance that we loaded the family through the opposite door."

"No one had inspected the car for a bomb?"

"They did. That doesn't mean anything in the game of warfare though. For all we know, someone on the security team could have planted it after the inspection. It was a typical device to blow up the gas tank and cause an inferno. The bomb wasn't complicated and didn't require much explosive to get the job done."

"What else did you learn at the hospital, Mack?" she asked as she swiveled her body to face him again.

The curtain fell to obscure the moon, and he leaned against the wall. "I learned that I wasn't the only one hurt. Cal and Eric were also in the hospital. Both of my lower legs were damaged by shrapnel. The nerves in my legs that control my feet were severed or damaged. It took too long to get me into surgery and the ischemia set in. They tried transferring the nerve, but it was too scarred down and didn't take. My time in the army was over."

"I still can't figure out what part of that makes you a coward, Mack. You did your job and paid a high price for something someone else did."

"I didn't go back for them, Charlotte. Right or wrong, I should have gone back."

"You should have gone back to a burning car to do what? Watch the fire? Get burned? What could you do when one glance told you they were dead?"

"They weren't just dead. The fire was so hot they had evaporated. I knew it. I'd seen it before. I still should have gone back."

"Here's the thing, Mack," she whispered, planting her hands on her hips. "Could have. Should have. Would have. Those are dangerous statements. They're all past tense. There's no rewind and replay in life. There's only did and did not."

"I did not do my job. There's your truth."

"Wrong. You did not die. That's the real truth here, Mack. Those people did, and you did not. This isn't about the decisions you made after the explosion. As humans, when we're faced with situations like those, trained or untrained, we can't predict what we will do. In a split second, you knew those people were gone, but your team was in danger. You didn't even know you were hurt in those first few seconds, did you?" He shook his head but kept his lips pursed, so he didn't argue with her about how wrong she was. "Adrenaline and fear are highly motivating to the human mind, Mack. Toss in the shock of a sudden injury, and the rule book goes out the window. Let me ask you a question?" He nodded, and she stood, walking over to him and standing directly in front of him. "What did the rest of your team do?"

"I told you. My team grabbed me and dragged me out of there. Eric picked us up in his truck and raced us to a waiting chopper."

"Did any of them run toward the burning car, Mack?"

He paused, holding her gaze as his mind returned to the heat and the noise that day. "Cal and Roman were in the front vehicle alone. They were out of their truck and securing the area. Eric and a second team were in a vehicle behind us when the explosion happened. I remember Eric drove around the car and picked us all up."

"Then, from what I'm hearing, you had a full team in two different vehicles, but none of them approached the car either?"

"Not that I remember. In the report, Eric said the fire was so hot they could feel the heat inside their truck as they passed it."

"Did the report say if Eric stopped to check on the occupants?"

"He didn't. He followed Cal's directive to abandon the mission."

"So why, in light of all that, do you feel like a coward? Were you the mission leader?" He shook his head, his jaw pulsing with anger and fear. The terror from that day filled him again, and he clenched his hands into fists to stop them from trembling. "Have you ever considered that no matter what choices you made that day, you couldn't have saved those people? Have you ever considered that it was beyond your pay grade and your control? Has anyone told you that it wasn't your fault? I'm telling you now. It wasn't your fault, Mack. You did your job, and the scars you carry are proof of that. You can't control the way that day changed your body or your mind. I understand that more than anyone, but the guilt is too heavy when it's not yours to carry."

Mack sucked air in through his nostrils and stared her down. "I guess I could say the same to you, Charlotte, but I suspect you'd tell me our situations were different, and you can't compare them. You'd be right. No one died because you didn't do your job. People died because I didn't do mine."

Before she could say anything, he pushed past her and walked out the door. He'd do well to remember that before Charlotte joined Secure One, his singular focus had been to help people in bad situations or protect them from bad people. He'd lost sight of that momentarily when Charlotte came into his life, but it was time he focused on that again. Doing anything else made him think he had a chance at a different life. He knew the truth. Being alone was his path in life. He had to make her understand that before she too became a casualty of his war.

MACK STARED OUT the cabin's window at the tumultuous water of the Mississippi, hoping it would help him sort out the noise in his head. What did Charlotte know about war? Nothing. She knew nothing. At least nothing about the kind of war he fought, right?

Mack walked over to Eric, who had been watching him pace. "Hey," he said, but Eric held his fingers in front of him, wagged them for a second, then punched around on his phone.

That was the sign for *hang on*, which Eric used when his hearing aids weren't connected properly. His hearing had been damaged in the same botched transport that injured Mack's legs. Without his hearing aids, he was legally deaf. Thankfully, he had the best of the best in aids to help him hear.

"Sorry, I had to disconnect the phone's Bluetooth from my hearing aids. What's up?"

"Checking in. Who were you talking to?"

"Cal," he said, holding up the phone before he pocketed it. "They're landing soon."

"Good, with any luck, we can try to make sense of this newest development. How is she?" Mack motioned at the door where Bethany slept.

"Charlotte stayed with her until she fell asleep. I'm supposed to tell her if Bethany wakes up, but she's out."

Mack grunted, frustration evident in the sound. Something had to break soon, or another woman was going to die. Frustration was all he felt tonight, both with the case and Charlotte.

"What crawled up your pants leg?" Eric asked, turning to him.

"Nothing. I'm frustrated with how nothing makes sense in this case."

"No, you're frustrated with how long it's taking to move on it."

"I'd like to figure it out before another woman dies, Eric."

"So would I, but in the end, we have one hand tied trying to work around the authorities. It will take more time when we don't have access to all the evidence."

Swiping his hand through his hair, Mack buried his fingers and left them there, his elbow swinging in the air. "I know, but I don't have to like it."

"Can't say that I do either."

"What do you remember about that day that ended our

service career?" Mack asked out of the blue, his trained eye noticing Eric's shoulders stiffen.

"You're asking what haunts me about it, right?" Eric asked, and Mack gave half a nod. "I vividly remember the back door cracking open and a little leg coming out right before the car exploded."

Mack glanced at him sharply. "You could see who opened the door?"

"I don't know if the boy opened it, but he would be the first one out. He probably was the one to open it. He was enamored with you, remember? He may not have understood the stay-in-the-car order."

"I never knew that," Mack said with a shudder. "I don't think it makes me feel better about it either."

"I didn't think it would, which is why I never told you. I also remember seeing you walk toward Cal, and then you just disappeared. I thought you dropped when the car exploded."

"I did, just not by choice."

"It wasn't until I got the truck around the burning car that I realized you were hurt."

"So were you."

"I didn't know that at the time. Getting you to a helo was our priority."

Mack shook his head with frustration. "Cal, me, you, all injured for nothing. I failed to do my job, and people were maimed and killed. Such a waste."

"You didn't fail to do your job."

Mack's snort was loud and sarcastic. "You and Charlotte."

"Charlotte doesn't know the first thing about war."

"Civilized warfare is still warfare, and the streets aren't

always civilized, Eric." Mack's tone was defensive, and Eric noticed.

"You're saying she knows a lot about war, just not your war."

With a finger pointed at his friend, Mack nodded. "When she was on the streets, she was an army of one. She was the only one who needed to walk away alive and unhurt. I had an entire team I let down when that mission went sideways."

"I never could figure out why you took that blame when there was never any blame to be had. You followed protocol by exiting the vehicle and taking your position before security inside the car led the family from the vehicle. We'd done it a dozen times the same way. It was unfortunate circumstances that weren't your fault. You didn't put that bomb in the car."

His chest was heavy when he let out a breath. Unfortunate circumstances that weren't his fault. Maybe that was true. Even if he couldn't control them, he still carried the scars from them.

"Listen, Mack, none of us escaped that mission without guilt. I think about that little foot sticking out every night when I go to bed. I have to remind myself that they were never getting out alive regardless of what we did. More of us would be dead if you opened that door at the airport rather than the other side. Stop feeling guilty. Nothing you did would have saved that family, but you did save many other people from dying. I know it will never fade away, just like all the other carnage we saw and participated in, but it's been too many years for you to let it control your life. I know that's easier said than done, but it's time to try."

"I've tried for years, Eric. I'm exhausted from trying."

Eric turned and crossed his arms over his chest, facing Mack with determination in his stance. "No, you haven't. You find it easier to deal with your disability by pretending it's your fault, but it's not. It's time you try to find some happiness in life, Mack. You don't even have to look for it. Happiness is waiting downstairs, but you're too dense to see it. It might be easier to let your past fade if you had someone to share your future with."

"Charlotte?" Eric's head tipped to the left slightly. "It's not like that, man. I'm part of her life to teach her how to trust again. That's it. That's all it can be."

"What a shame," Eric said, dropping his arms to his sides. "She smooths out your rough edges. I'll go prepare the rest of the security team for Cal's arrival. You're on bodyguard duty until I get back."

The treads of his boots made a hiss on the wood floor as he walked away, leaving Mack to stare at the wall. Eric's words echoed in his ears.

She smooths out your rough edges.

She absolutely did, but he'd never ask a woman like Charlotte to tie herself to a guy like him. His demons took up too much space and left no room for love.

Chapter Eleven

"Charlotte?"

Surprised by the intrusion, she spun around to see Mina standing in the doorway. She wore her Secure One uniform with a gun on her hip and her running blade prosthesis strapped inside a tennis shoe. Mina had several prostheses, but when working a job, she always wore the one that made her the fastest.

"Mina!" Before she could say another word, she was wrapped in a warm hug from her friend. "I'm so glad you're here."

"I was the first one on the helicopter. I heard Bethany's voice, and it sent a shiver down my spine. How is she?"

"She's sleeping after she had something to eat. Eric and Mack are taking turns on guard duty. Bethany is beyond exhausted. She'll need a lot of help if she's going to have a life after what she's been through."

"There are resources out there for women like her. We'll get the information we need from her and then, depending on what she tells us, protect her or find her someplace with the services she needs. Until I hear her story, I won't know which one comes first."

Charlotte nodded after ending the hug. "The only thing she told me before she fell asleep was that she escaped someone who had been holding her hostage. She ran, stole a truck and rode a bus to get here."

"But how did she know about here?" Cal asked, walking through the open door with Roman.

"Hey, guys," Charlotte said, her gaze flicking to Mina for a moment, who nodded for her to answer. "She escaped the night we found Layla on the shore. She had the radio on and heard them talking about Secure One finding the body. They also mentioned we'd been involved in the death of The Miss. Since she had no other choice, she made her way here by bus and on foot, hoping she could find us."

"She sounds like a real spitfire," Cal said, bouncing up on his toes. "I know a couple of other women like her too. I can't wait to meet her."

"She's precarious, Cal," Charlotte warned him.

"Meaning?"

"Meaning she's been through hell, and we need to ask questions that don't push her over the razor-thin edge she's on."

"We understand that," Roman said. "Selina and Marlise are upstairs with her right now. Selina is going to check her over in case she needs a hospital. Marlise is there as a familiar face."

"I could have gone up. You didn't need to drag Marlise here," Charlotte said defensively.

Cal held out his hand to hush her. "I need you here to walk me through what we have before they bring Bethany down. You're in the thick of this case, and I need your insight."

Mack strode into the room then and didn't stop until he stood behind her. His hands went to her shoulders as though he noticed her tension. "Everything okay?"

"Fine," Cal assured him. "We were just talking about Bethany and the case. Charlotte is upset, which is completely understandable. This case gets more and more disturbing every day."

Mack rubbed her shoulders up and down as he spoke. "Agreed, and we don't even know if Bethany's situation is tied to The Red River Slayer."

"That's why we're here," Mina said, setting her bag up on the desk. "We can work remotely, and we will, but first, I wanted to talk to everyone in person. That way, I can start a more focused dive into our evidence when I get back to Secure One."

"You mean so you can hack the right agency to get more information," Mack said, tongue in cheek.

"You say potato," Mina answered with a grin.

She unloaded her pack and set up her computer while Cal and Roman taped Charlotte's map to the office wall.

Mack leaned into her ear and whispered, "We'll talk later about earlier."

His breath blew across her skin and raised goose bumps along her neck that she couldn't hide or deny. Why did his simple words and actions raise such a response in her? She was trying hard not to like him, but he wasn't making it easy. What he was doing was making it easy to fall into his arms and let him protect her. She couldn't let that happen though. If she was going to take back her life and find success, it would be because she worked hard. If she let someone else save her every time, that didn't teach her how to take care of herself.

What if he doesn't want to save you as much as he wants to love you?

Absolutely not. Charlotte shut that voice down without

hesitation. There was no way she was falling for Mack. Her gaze flicked to Cal at the board, and she wondered how he made it work with Marlise. They lived and worked together all day, every day, but their relationship felt seamless. Her wayward gaze drifted to Mack, who had stepped back to the door to guard it as everyone prepared for the meeting. He was a giant. As much in kindness, empathy and understanding as he was in size. An unfamiliar heat flickered through her. She suspected it was the flame she would carry for this man forever. She'd never been with a man who didn't want something from her. Every man she'd encountered had an ulterior motive behind taking care of her, being with her, dating her or taking advantage of her. There had never been anyone in her life like Mack.

Safe.

Part of her believed that word, but the rest knew he wasn't safe. At least to her heart. He made it feel things it shouldn't, and that made him dangerous. Her therapist told her it was okay to want that kind of life, but she wasn't sure she deserved it. She had done things— illegal things—that harmed others. The drugs she ferried for The Madame probably killed people. She was the kind of person Mack actively worked to put behind bars. Maybe she hadn't done those things willingly, but she'd still done them.

"This is a mess," Cal said where he stood by the map. "The case, I mean. It's not even our case, but we're still in the middle of it."

Eric walked in at that moment and stood at the back by Mack. Charlotte could see that he was tired, they all were, but until this case was solved, no one was getting much sleep.

"All we can do is work the evidence, Cal," Mina said from behind her computer. "That's the only way out of this mess."

"We keep saying that, but it never happens," Roman pointed out, leaning on the desk next to his wife. "It feels like that game *Whac-A-Mole*. We knock one bad girl down, and another one pops up."

"Or, in this case, a bad boy," Mack said from the doorway while motioning at the map on the wall.

"Could still be a bad girl," Roman said with a shrug.

"You think this is tied to Red Rye?" Eric asked. Charlotte could hear the skepticism in his voice, but she had none in her mind.

"I don't know if it's tied directly to Red Rye, but it could be tied to the business The Madame had going at the time."

"The first bodies were found while you were all at Red Rye." Cal pointed at the six rivers where the original women were found. "That's a little suspect if you ask me."

"Especially when you consider what SAC Moore told me the night he kidnapped me," Mina said, glancing at Roman.

"What did he tell you?" Cal asked.

"That Liam Albrecht had some serious kinks, and The Miss had to do cleanup on more than one occasion."

Cal took a step toward the desk. "You could have mentioned that sooner."

Mina shrugged. "It just crossed my mind again when you said the first bodies were all from Red Rye. Maybe The Miss cleaned those women up by passing them off to someone else to do the deed rather than do it herself. We know it wasn't Liam killing the women because he's dead, and we're still finding them."

"But, of the recent women found, only one didn't have an identity, and that was the last one," Mack said, walking to the front of the room.

"Layla," Charlotte said through gritted teeth. "Her name was Layla, and she was just a scared young woman who didn't deserve to die that way."

Mina held up her hand. "The FBI knows her identity. They just haven't released her name yet."

Mack kept his hand on the small of her back to calm her. "Okay, so now we know all the women from this killing spree were identified."

"Which makes sense," Cal said. "There aren't many washed women left from The Madame's empire."

"No, but he's still taking throwaway women," Mina said from behind her computer. "Our perp chooses victims from the street because homeless people always move around. Even if she had friends on the street, they wouldn't think anything of her going missing."

"And even if they did, the police aren't going to spend time looking for her," Charlotte added. Her voice was thin, tired and exhausted from life, which made her appreciate Mack's strong but caring touch on her back even more. "We know he's not impulsive. He's taking the time to pick the right women and not just grabbing random ones."

"He might even get off on the hunt," Eric said as he walked to the front of the room to sit. "He probably watched each victim for days. Learned their routine. Decided if anyone would notice that her things were there, but she wasn't. He may even watch her long enough to know what things are important to her and makes sure he grabs her when she has those items. That makes it look to her friends like she just took off."

"Or he just grabs the first street woman he sees. We have twelve bodies, but that doesn't mean that all the victims have been found," Cal reminded everyone. "There could be more victims who never floated to shore."

"All true," Mina agreed, typing away on her computer. "I've had my ear to the ground for bodies of drowning victims found anywhere during the two years between Red Rye and now."

"Nothing, right?" Eric asked, but Mina stuck her head around the computer and shook it.

"Actually, no. Two more women were found, but they didn't fare well in the water. A gator probably attacked one, and one was caught in a dam for some time. No ability to run facial recognition and no recognizable marks to tell a family if it was their missing child. The police couldn't say it was The Red River Slayer, so they didn't."

"They weren't strangled?" Mack asked from next to her. A shiver ran through Charlotte, and he rubbed it away with his hand on her back.

"No way to know. Their heads were either gone or damaged in a way that could have caused the trauma. DNA identification will take a significant amount of time."

"Do you know what rivers?" Cal asked, walking to the giant map Charlotte had drawn.

Mina held up a finger and typed more on the computer before answering. "The Savannah River, which explains the gator attack, and the Colorado River."

"We have a victim in the Colorado already," Cal said, putting his finger on the *X* Charlotte had made on the map.

"We do," Charlotte agreed, moving to the front of the room. She took the marker from Cal, "but that doesn't mean anything. The Colorado runs through like, what?"

She paused and counted on the map. "Seven states. The first victim in that river was found in the state of Colorado. Mina, what state was this woman found in?"

"Arizona," she answered. "They think she was caught in the Glen Canyon Dam."

"That's not too far from where we found The Miss," Mack pointed out.

"And we're back to whether this is tied to The Madame," Cal said with frustration.

"I can say it's always in the back of my mind," Mack said. "It's possible someone was killing The Madame's women, and that was why bodies were being found during that time. Then The Madame was on trial, and rather than draw unwanted attention to himself, he stuck a pin in the business until things quieted down."

"The only tie we have is that some of the women killed worked for her. That could be a coincidence."

"Could be," Cal agreed, "but it's not. The Red River Slayer could have started as a client or a fan of what The Madame was doing, but he quickly became a psychopathic serial killer. Regardless of whether he or she was mixed up with the Red Rye fiasco, we need to move that to the back burner while we try to find him."

"Agreed," Eric said from his seat, "but we don't know how to find him."

"Or why someone tried to kidnap Ella the other night," Charlotte added.

"The more I think about it, the more I don't think it's connected," Mack said. "I think the kidnapping had more to do with who her father is, and the attempted kidnapper thought the chaos of that night was a good way to grab the girl without notice."

"And do what with her?" Charlotte asked. "Hold her hostage?"

"Ransom," Mina said from the computer. "Dorian would pay anything to get his daughter back."

"Which brings us back to whether the river slayings are politically driven. I'll need to plot the other bodies in what state and town they were found. Based on Ella's theory that killings have to do with senators seeking re-election, we have to ask ourselves two questions. First, did the killer take a break during those two years because the elections were over? Second, did he take a break for a different reason?"

"Or if he was practicing his technique and we just haven't found the bodies. He may have been preparing for when this election cycle came around." Mina stood and motioned at the map. "A sixteen-year-old girl came up with it as soon as it was laid out on paper. We should have."

"We're not in the business of politics or solving murders, Mina. Ella is immersed in politics, so to her, it was obvious. *If* that's the motivating factor," Cal reminded her.

"When will the police release Layla's sketch to the public?" Charlotte asked. "It's been radio silence for days."

"They're not going to," Cal answered. "They know who she is already, and their theory is every time they release information about the river slayings, they're giving the killer airtime, which is what he wants."

"But she deserves justice!" Charlotte exclaimed in anger.

Mina peeked around the computer again. "Layla didn't have a family, right?" Charlotte shook her head. "The police aren't hurting anything by keeping this under their hat then. From the perspective of a law enforcement agent, I understand what they're doing. As a woman, it angers me that they're stealing her justice."

"My fear is, not giving the guy airtime will result in another woman dying," Cal said with a sigh.

"We can't let that happen," Eric said, standing and grabbing a marker. "List off the senators up for reelection. I'm going to write them in their corresponding state."

Charlotte hadn't turned away from Mack. She was lost in the way his gaze calmed her pounding heart. She wanted to run from the room and the nightmare of this investigation, but he wouldn't let her. He would help her face her past to move on to a better future. That was all she wanted, but it couldn't be with him. Not to be cliché, but he deserved better, and she knew it. Her entire life went against his code of ethics. She was what he was trying to stop by fighting for this country.

"Ron Dorian, Minnesota. Pete Fuller, South Carolina. Greg Weiss, Maine," Roman was reading off the computer when Mina stood up with a gasp.

"Greg Weiss?" She lowered herself to the chair again and looked at the other computer that Roman was on.

"Do you know him?" Mack asked.

She stood but shook her head with confusion. "He was friends with the two guys The Madame killed in the warehouse the night she kidnapped me. I found his name several times tied to Red Rye. I assumed he knew Liam Albrecht, the city manager for Red Rye, because they were all involved in politics."

"Was there evidence that he was involved with any women in the Red Rye house?"

"None," Mina said. "He knew Albrecht, but that doesn't mean anything in the world of politics. It's all a game. He could have been working them for money for his campaign, or they were friends through an organization. I was never able to sort out their exact relationship."

"Another point in the Red Rye column," Mack said. "Is that all of them, Roman?"

"Yes, for the current cycle. A third of the senate is re-elected every two years—this year, there are thirty-three. If we remove the eight women found, including the two who they aren't sure about, from the last election cycle, only six of the thirty-three states have a dead body." Eric put a check next to the senators from each state that already had a victim. "I'm afraid many more women will be killed if this is politically motivated."

Selina walked in the door at that moment, and everyone turned to her. "Sorry to interrupt, but I can't put Bethany through anything more tonight with good conscience. Her body and mind aren't even working together anymore since she's so exhausted. I can barely rouse her long enough to do her vitals."

Everyone looked at each other and waited for Cal to speak. When he did, it was no surprise what he said. "Then we give her until morning. It's already midnight, so a few more hours won't break the bank. We're rested and will take over security duty so Eric, Mack and Charlotte can get some rest. Selina, you and Marlise stay with Bethany. Roman, you and I will pull guard duty. Mina, can you keep working on this?"

He got a thumbs-up from behind her computer, but she barely broke stride in her typing long enough to give it.

"We'll reconvene here at seven a.m. unless something arises beforehand. We will have to talk to Bethany at that point," Cal said to Selina. "When most of the team is here, the rest of the team at Secure One is in a bind."

"Understood," Selina said. "I think a good stretch of sleep will be enough to help her mind put everything in order. This poor woman was held hostage for nearly two years. Everyone needs to understand that she may or may not have answers, but once we're done talking to her, I have to check her into a facility that can take care of her mental and emotional wounds besides her physical ones."

"That is heard and understood," Cal said. "She came to us, which means she wanted to tell us something. That's the only reason I'm staying here other than to give the team a break. Honestly, I need more help than I have right now. We're stretched too thin."

"I know a guy," Mina said, popping up.

"You know a guy?" Mack asked with a chuckle. "Is he trustworthy?"

"He's an amp friend. He did a tour for the army in the sandbox and lost his left leg but earned a purple heart and a medal of honor for saving two guys even as he was bleeding out. Rehabbed and returned for a tour in the mountains, this time as private security since the government said no to a second tour."

"Private security meaning mercenary," Mack muttered.

"Call him whatever you want. He won't care. He's stateside now and working private security as a bodyguard."

"A bodyguard who's an amp?" Eric asked with a raised brow.

"He can do more on one leg than you can do with both of your own. He can overtake you in seconds when he puts on his running blade. He runs marathons for fun on the weekend. I wouldn't hesitate to let him protect me."

"Does he have a name?" Cal asked, his tone holding interest.

"Efren."

"Sounds like he'd fit in well here. Give him a call. See if he's available. Run our standard background on him. I know you know him, but he has to align with our clearances for our clients."

"On it," she said, sitting again.

"The rest of you find an empty room and get some sleep. It might be your only chance for a few more days."

Charlotte feared he was right, so she headed to the room where she'd left her bag. She was going to grab a shower and some shut-eye. She made sure not to make eye contact with Mack when she left the room. He may want to talk about what happened earlier, but she did not. She planned to be asleep before he ever found her.

Chapter Twelve

Mack's hand rested on the doorknob, and he took a deep breath. It was time to clear the air with Charlotte. He turned the knob and pushed the door open just a crack. He put his lips to the opening to speak. "Char, it's Mack. I'm coming in."

He stood by the door and waited for a response that didn't come. Charlotte was fooling herself if she thought he'd go away if she pretended to be asleep. He stepped into the room and turned the light on next to the bed, expecting to see her there. She wasn't. Fear lanced his chest. Where was she? Had someone gotten to her?

A sound came from the bathroom, and he let out a sigh. His heart was pounding as he lowered himself to the bed and braced his hands on his knees. This case was getting to him, and so was this woman. He was about to do something he'd never done before, and the mere idea of being that open with someone scared him.

The bathroom door opened, and he lifted his head to come face-to-face with Char wrapped in a towel and nothing else. Her long hair was damp around the edges but hung free without a tie.

"Mack? Wha—what are you doing in here?" He noticed

her hands pull the towel a little tighter around herself, but it was too late. He was already imagining her without it.

"We need to talk, Char."

"Not tonight, Mack. We're both tired, and Cal is giving us a chance to get some sleep."

"This won't take long," he promised, standing and taking the robe off the bathroom door. He held it out for Charlotte to slip her arms in, and she stared him down for a solid minute before she turned her back and slid one arm into the robe. She grasped the towel with that hand and slipped her other one in, tying it around her before letting the towel fall.

She may be good at keeping herself hidden, but he saw her and liked all of her. She was wrong if she thought he didn't notice her beautiful skin that glowed in the light of the lamp or the swell of her breasts from under the towel. He noticed all of her, the good and what she thought was bad, but he knew he wanted all of her. He was positive convincing Char of that would be more difficult than it should be.

He hung the towel on the bathroom doorknob and motioned for her to sit on the bed. "What do you want, Mack?" she asked, her fingers toying with the bathrobe's belt.

"I want to talk. You said could have, should have and would have are dangerous because they're past tense."

Char lifted her gaze to his. "So?"

"I talked to Eric, and he said some things that surprised me about the mission that day."

"Things like it wasn't your fault, and you did nothing wrong?"

"That and how others could have died, including me,

had I opened the other door to load the family for the transport."

"I suppose he's not wrong," she agreed. "I hadn't thought of that."

"Surprisingly, during all these years, neither had I. There were so many situations in that sandbox that should have killed me. Do you know about Hannah?"

"Cal's girlfriend in the army?" she asked, and he nodded. "Marlise told me she was killed, and Cal was shot."

"I was there. I killed the insurgent who was firing those bullets at my friends. Cal recovered and returned to the team, but he was never the same. Then the transport happened, and we all left for good."

"And started Secure One. There were worse things you could have done, Mack."

"Cal started Secure One," he clarified. "First, he worked as a mercenary and weapons expert for a few years while I wallowed."

"You wallowed?"

"In self-pity," he said, leaning down and loosening the laces on his boots. He lifted his pant leg, loosened the Velcro strap around his calf, and pulled his foot out. Immediately, his toes pointed to the floor while he pulled the sock off. He did the same on the other side until both feet were sock free and resting on the floor. "I went from running miles daily to barely walking to the bathroom with a walker, Char. The self-pity was strong, but the self-hatred was stronger. It was Cal and Eric who finally forced me to face the truth. This was my life now." He motioned at his feet, then lifted them up again. They hung down, his big toes touching the floor. "No amount of working out will make my feet move again. No matter how long

I stare at them, I'll never be able to raise my toes off the floor the way you do. Willpower won't make the muscles, nerves and tendons all work together again. I had to face the truth, accept it and move forward with the hand I'd been dealt. Or in this case, foot."

She turned to face him. "You're trying to say I need to accept my past so I can find a new life."

"No, not at all," he said with a shake of his head. "I'm trying to say it's okay to want a new life. For the longest time, I thought these scars held me back from life. Then I turned the scars around and used them for good."

"They reminded you that there are bad people in the world who need to be stopped." He nodded, and she couldn't hide her grimace. "That's the problem, Mack. I'm one of those bad people you've worked to stop."

He tipped her chin up with his finger until she was forced to hold his gaze. "That's not true, Char. You're not a bad person."

"I've done a lot of bad things. Things that go against who you are and what you believe, Mack. I've run drugs, been an escort and even had to, you know."

Her gaze hit the floor again, and he rested his forehead against hers. "I do know, but the difference is you didn't do any of those things because you wanted to. You did those things because you had to. I understand the difference, Char. The fact that you're here tonight tells me that you're inherently a good person. You want to help others and rid the world of people like The Madame who prey on innocent people."

"I do, but I still did those other things, Mack. Being with someone like me goes against everything you believe in."

He was silent, simply gazing into her eyes from where he rested against her forehead. "Did you want to do those things?"

"Of course not!" she exclaimed, jumping up and falling into the bathroom door. Mack steadied her, but she ripped her elbow from his grip to walk to the chair in the corner. "I did what I had to do to survive."

He moved his boots aside and stood, readying himself for something he'd never done before. He was about to be vulnerable with someone he only wanted to be strong for. He took an exaggerated step, lifting his thigh high to clear the floor of his toes that hung down. His foot made a "thwap" as it landed back on the hardwood floor. The same happened with the other leg, back and forth, until he stood before her.

"That's all any of us can do, Char. I don't believe in killing people, but I still had to do it in the army. I'm technically a murderer. Does that mean I'm a bad person?"

"No," she whispered, staring at her lap. "You were protecting innocent people and us at home, Mack. Nothing you did in the service can be considered bad if you followed orders."

"Then I say we level the playing field when it comes to you and me." He sat on the ottoman in front of her and took her hands.

"How?" she asked, lifting her head to gaze into his eyes. He got so lost in the depths of her blue ones that he fought to answer her.

"We consider ourselves equals."

"But we're not!" she exclaimed. "You're so much more than I am, Mack. You deserve so much more than I can offer you in this life. You need to leave, please."

She hung her head again, but he didn't leave. He leaned forward and did what he'd wanted to do since he first laid eyes on her. He kissed her. Her lips were soft, and she tasted of stolen innocence. She went stock still the moment their lips connected. He waited, his lips on hers, to see if she would find a way past her fear to enjoy the kiss. He worried she would force herself to kiss him because that was what she thought she had to do. He wanted the first, but if the second happened, he'd stop the kiss until she learned the difference.

Instead, she pulled away and brought her hands to her lips. "What are you doing?"

"Kissing you," he answered. The truth was simple. It was the acceptance that was hard.

"Why?"

"I want to, Char. I've wanted to kiss you since the day I met you."

"You're just saying that to get me to kiss you back."

His sigh was heavy when he shook his head. "No, I'm not, but I understand why you feel that way. It's hard to be vulnerable." He held up his pants legs to show her the scars, pitting and missing flesh from his calves. "But being vulnerable also requires bravery and courage. I didn't want to take my boots off and show you these scars. I'm as vulnerable as I can get when my legs are bare. It's hard to trust someone with the parts of you that you're ashamed of, but sometimes, the right person teaches you how to accept them and lose the shame."

He stood and walked to the bed, his high steppage gait leaving a slapping sound on the floor with every footfall. He bent, picked up his boots in one hand and grabbed the bedpost to steady himself.

"Where are you going?"

"To my room to get some sleep, you should too."

Mack took two steps and stopped when she moved in front of the door. "You aren't going to try to kiss me again?"

"No, Char. The next time I kiss you, it will be because you asked me to."

She was silent, and they faced off. Mack could see the turmoil in her eyes. For a moment, he felt terrible for putting it there. Then that emotion disappeared, and a new one replaced it. Pride. He had given her something to think about—she could change her life if she found a way to be vulnerable again. It wouldn't be easy for her after what she'd been through, but she would be better because of it.

"Aren't you going to put your boots on? You never let anyone see you without them."

Mack glanced down at the boots and then back to her. "No. I'm no longer ashamed of my legs, Char. Your drawing was the reason I could be vulnerable here tonight. When I saw the expression you'd drawn, it was how I feel inside every day. That's the fear I have of someone thinking I'm less because of these. The words you wrote about my legs were validation about something I couldn't change. If I couldn't change it, I shouldn't feel ashamed." He walked to the door and turned the knob when she stepped out of the way. "Thank you for giving me that little piece of myself back. I'd love to have the drawing when and if you're ready to part with it. Get some sleep, Char. Tomorrow will be another long day."

He bent down and kissed her cheek before he left her room and walked down the hallway, waiting to hear her shut the door. She never did.

Chapter Thirteen

Sleep wouldn't come no matter what. Charlotte had been in bed for almost two hours but kept falling into short dreams about Mack, where all his pain and life experiences hung from him like appendages. It was disturbing, and she finally sat up and tossed her feet over the bed. She needed to walk off some nervous energy, or she'd never sleep. It was almost 3:00 a.m., so the grounds would be quiet. Maybe she'd walk down to the river and breathe the fresh air to clear her head.

After dressing, she slipped down the darkened hallways to avoid the guards stationed at the doorways. She didn't want anyone tagging along with her outside. She wanted to stand by the water and decide if Mack was right. Did vulnerability do the opposite of what you expected it to do?

She stepped outside and walked across the lawn toward the river, wishing it were true, but in her case, there was no way to vanquish the shame she carried. It filled every gaping hole in her soul and filtered into every crack and crevice. No, vulnerability could not take her shame away. That was something she would have to live with forever.

She stepped onto the dock and walked to the end, looking out over the dark flowing water. A tear fell down her cheek as she pictured Mack taking his boots off and walking toward her. It wasn't pity making her cry, but instead that he put himself out there, and she pushed him away. Her fingers brushed her lips where he'd kissed her. For a split second, she was terrified, but then a different sensation took over. After Mack left her room, it took her a long time to understand that his kiss showed her how much he cared. Mack wasn't there for a quick roll in the hay. He was there because he cared deeply about her.

Charlotte thought back over her life but couldn't think of another man who had made her feel that way. For the most part, men were indifferent to her unless they thought they could somehow use her to better their position. That was certainly true during her time with The Madame. The expression on Mack's face as he told her that her drawing gave him the courage to be vulnerable held nothing but honesty. That wasn't lip service. He meant it. He'd shown it by holding his head high as he left the room, no longer hiding his disability.

"Secure two, Whiskey," came a voice from behind her, and Charlotte jumped, spinning around to face Mina as she walked down the dock.

"Mina, you scared me."

"Imagine if I'd been someone out to do you harm. You wouldn't have seen them coming."

"How did you find me out here?" Charlotte discreetly wiped her eyes while she waited for an answer. Mina was right. She hadn't been paying attention, and that could have been deadly. *Damn you, Mack Holbock, and your ridiculously soft lips.*

"Cameras cover this entire property. Or did you forget?"

A groan left Charlotte's lips as her chin fell to her chest. "I just wanted to be alone. I forgot about the cameras."

"That's why I gave you some time. There aren't many reasons for a single woman to be out here at this time of night unless she needs to be alone. Mack?"

She gave her friend a shoulder shrug as she leaned on the deck railing.

"Listen, let me give you a little piece of advice. It's time to take your power back, Charlotte. If you don't, you'll find yourself standing in this same place year after year, wondering why life isn't working out for you."

"How do I take my power back when I never had any to begin with?" Charlotte was angry, and she balled her hands into fists at her sides.

"You're wrong. You are the only one with the power when it comes to yourself. That's the first thing you do to take power back. You stop blaming everyone else for where you are in life."

"But it's their fault!"

Mina held up her hand to calm her. "I know it's their fault. Everyone in your life did you wrong. There's no question. But blame is like poison. The longer you swallow it, the more toxic it becomes and the weaker you get. Letting go of the blame and starting fresh from where you are today gives you back all the power they took from you."

Charlotte stared at Mina for a long moment and then tipped her head. "I guess that kind of makes sense."

"It makes a lot of sense and will be easier to say than do. I get that. You have to trust yourself. Just the way you did the other night when you didn't hesitate to defend Ella. Confidence in who you are as a person helps you let the blame go."

"I don't have a lot of confidence. I never have."

"That's the whole idea of reclaiming your power, Char-

lotte. You picture yourself as the beautiful, strong, coura-
geous and brave woman we all see rather than what all the
toxic people in your life said you were. Once you do that
consistently, you have all the control again. Do the things
that make you feel powerful, even if that means you take
those things back from the toxic people too."

"Like art?" Charlotte leaned against the railing and
wiped her face one more time of a wayward tear that refused to stay behind her lid.

"Yes, like art. I'm not going to tell you to go out and
start tagging buildings again," Mina said with a lip tilt
that made Charlotte laugh. "But you can use your art to
do good the same as you have been with Secure One. The
map you drew for Mack to help him visualize the rivers across the country was so intricate and defined that
it blew my computer-based model out of the water. See
what I did there?"

A smile tilted Charlotte's lips up, and she nodded. "Well
done. I'm glad I can use my only talent to help others."

"Wrong," Mina said instantly. "You have so many more
talents than art. You just made my point. You're listening
to the toxic people from your past rather than trusting in
what you know about yourself."

After sharing a moment of silence, Charlotte could see
her point. "You're right. Why do I do that? I'm free now.
I should be celebrating that and moving forward rather
than keeping myself locked in that past." Mina nodded and
gave her a playful punch on the arm. Charlotte groaned
and let her head fall backward. "I screwed up tonight."

"With Mack?"

"How did you know?"

"Woman's intuition," she answered with a wink. Then

she hooked Charlotte's arm in hers, and they walked back toward the house. "You can fix it."

"You don't know what happened."

"I don't need to know," she promised, her head swiveling as they walked across the grass toward the house. "I can see the emotion that flows between you when you're together. There will be fits and starts to any relationship, especially with your complicated past, but if you're honest with him, things will smooth out."

Mina held the door open, and Charlotte walked back to her room in a daze. Did she want a relationship with Mack? When she picked up her drawing pad and opened it, the truth was there in black and white.

AFTER A SHOWER and coffee, Mack was still tired. Try as he might, sleep hadn't come easily. He knew he'd done the right thing with Charlotte, even if it hadn't been the easy thing. Now he had to get his head in the game and work this case before another woman died—a woman just like Charlotte.

Wrong. A woman like Charlotte used to be.

The voice was right. Charlotte wasn't a helpless woman caught in dire circumstances anymore. She was an essential part of the team and didn't hesitate to jump into the fray for the good of others. He had to remember that. She didn't need to be saved.

"Everything quiet?" Mack asked Eric as he walked by Ella's room.

"There was a bit of a disturbance, but Mina took care of it." Mack cocked his head, and Eric's gaze drifted to the windows for a moment. "Charlotte went for a walk without telling anyone. Mina saw her on the cameras and pulled her back in."

A curse word fell from Mack's lips. "She knows better than to go out alone."

Eric held up his hands. "Take it up with her. They're in command central. Selina is preparing Bethany to bring her down."

"Are you coming down too?"

A shake of his head said that was a negative. "No one to put on Ella. We're too short-staffed."

"Bring her down."

"To command central?"

Mack shrugged. "Why not? Let's face it. She's already knee-deep in this sludge. Maybe listening to us will spark something she remembers about her dad and his campaign. If nothing else, she can be there for Bethany. We need you down there so you know what's going on."

"Ten-four. I'll prepare her and be down shortly."

Mack gave him a salute and jogged down the stairs toward the office. They needed a break on this case soon. He already knew what the police were doing, and the answer to that was nothing. Every day they wasted was another day closer to a woman's death. He doubted Bethany had anything to add as far as the river killings went, but she may be able to tie up The Madame's loose strings, including where the other three Misses had gone when they escaped the raids.

Voices drifted out of the control room, and Mack stopped next to the door and leaned on the frame, watching Charlotte at the whiteboard. She had a marker and was making lists next to her paper map. One was in blue, and one was in red. Mack recognized a few of the names on each list. They were the senators up for reelection.

"Good morning," Mack said, walking in the door as though he hadn't been standing there, watching her. "Everything quiet?"

"For now," Mina answered, her gaze flicking to Charlotte. "Just waiting on the rest of the team."

"I told Eric to bring Ella down with him. He needs to be in the loop, and she's up to her waist in this disaster anyway."

Mina stood and stretched. "I agree. Dorian may not, but we just won't tell him." Mack and Charlotte both laughed, but Mack let his die off just to hear Charlotte's. When she laughed, it felt like hope to him. "I'm going to get some coffee. Do you guys want anything?"

"I'd have a cup," Charlotte said. "Let me come with you."

Mina brushed her away with her hand and walked to the door. "I can handle two cups of coffee. I'll be back before everyone gets here."

The room was silent as Mack walked up to the board where Charlotte stood. "How did you sleep?" He brushed a piece of hair off her face and behind her ear.

"I didn't. How about you?"

"Equally as well. I heard you took a walk. You shouldn't do that right now."

To his surprise, she didn't drop her gaze or look away. She held him in her atmosphere as her spine stiffened, and she lifted her chin a hair. "I decide what I do, not you. I was perfectly safe, considering this place is a fortress."

Mack lifted a brow but bit back the need to point out that while they were there, Cal was in charge and gave the orders. He didn't say it because he liked her spunk.

She was holding onto the power she'd found within herself here, and he wasn't going to be the one to clip her wings.

Rather than say anything more, he motioned at the boards. "What's this?"

Charlotte smiled as though she were thankful for the subject change. "I was making a list of the senators running for reelection listed by the party. It's hard when they're all over the map. I thought it might help us recognize patterns or common denominators."

"Has it?"

"Not yet, but I just finished the list." She was laughing, and Mack ate up the sound. She didn't laugh freely that often, so when she did, he wanted to be there to hear it. "About last night," she whispered, staring over his shoulder. "I'm sorry for treating you the way I did. I was scared and didn't know how to react."

"I understood that," Mack promised, giving her a gentle hug. "Never apologize for standing up for yourself. You weren't ready, and you let me know that. I wasn't upset. I respect your boundaries, Char."

She sank into him as though those were the exact words she needed to hear.

Chapter Fourteen

"Charlotte?"

Mack and Charlotte jumped apart to see Bethany in the doorway with Marlise on one side and Selina on the other.

"Bethany." Charlotte walked to her and took her hand. "How are you doing?"

"I'm okay," she said with a smile. "Selina and Marlise have been taking good care of me. I'm sorry to scare you the way I did. I didn't know what else to do."

"Don't apologize," Charlotte said, giving her a gentle squeeze. "I wasn't scared as much as I was in shock that you were here. I worried so much about you and Emelia. To hear your voice was a shock."

"You worried about us? Even after what we did?"

Marlise and Selina led Bethany to a chair where she sat. Charlotte sat next to her and offered her a smile.

"You did what you thought you had to do to be free. I would never judge you for that, even if you saw overthrowing The Miss as your only option."

"That wasn't what we wanted to do!" she exclaimed. "We wanted to overthrow her, so we could let all the women go!"

"It's okay," Charlotte said, trying to calm her. "I believe you. There was no way for you to know that her father was running drugs into the states and funding her operation. Take a deep breath and try to stay calm. We want to hear your story, but we want everyone here, so let's wait for Cal and the rest of the team to arrive."

"Her father was supplying the drugs we had to move?"

"Yes," Charlotte said, squeezing her hand gently. "You never had a chance of overthrowing her. Her death was the only way to be free."

"And she's dead?" she asked, glancing between everyone, but Mack answered.

"She is. Unfortunately, I had to protect my team, and she was the casualty."

"Nothing unfortunate about that woman being dead." Her tone was firm and left no question regarding how she felt about the matter. "The Madame is in jail?"

"For a good long time," Charlotte assured her. "We don't have to worry about her anymore."

Mina walked in with a carafe of coffee while Cal and the rest of the team filtered in. After Mina handed out cups of coffee, everyone sat comfortably in a semicircle to hear what Bethany had to say. The discussion was being recorded in case there was information for the police. Mack was sure that would be their next step, but they'd listen to what she had to say since Bethany came to them first.

"Tell us what you remember about the last time you saw The Miss," Charlotte said. Cal had asked her to take the lead on questioning because the last thing they wanted to do was scare Bethany or make things harder for her. She had a story to tell. That was why she was here, but allowing her to tell it would be the trickiest part.

"After we talked to The Miss about our plan, it was late. She told us she'd think about making us more pivotal members of the team. Satisfied, we went to bed in our pod. When I woke up, I was in a basement bedroom. That's all I remember. I don't know how many days I was out or how I got there. I know it was a basement because the window was at the top of the room and I could see the ground at the window level. Before I had time to figure out what had happened, he walked in."

"He?" Charlotte asked. "Did he have a name?"

Bethany nodded but then shook her head. She finally shrugged as though she didn't know the answer. "He told me my new name was Angel and forced me to call him Little Daddy."

"Little Daddy? That's different. Usually, they just want to be called daddy," Charlotte said, taking Bethany's hand.

"Right?" she asked, trying to lighten the mood with girl banter, but it didn't hit the same way when you'd been held hostage for years by someone using the name Little Daddy. "But the thing is, there's a Big Daddy somewhere," she whispered, her words falling on each other out of fear. "When Little Daddy thinks you're ready, he sends you to Big Daddy."

"Did you ever meet Big Daddy?" Charlotte asked, and Bethany immediately began shaking her head.

She leaned in to whisper to Charlotte. "The night I escaped, Little Daddy told me I was ready for Big Daddy. That's when I knew I had to run."

"Running was the right thing to do, Bethany. Were you the only woman there? What happened to Emelia?"

"I don't know," she said as her voice broke. "When I woke up in the basement, she wasn't with me."

Mina glanced at Mack, and he knew what she was thinking. Was Emelia one of those unidentified women from two years ago? At this point, he'd believe anything was possible.

"You woke up almost eighteen months ago and were alone in the house?" Charlotte asked to clarify.

"In the beginning, another woman was there with me, but she didn't last very long before he took her to Big Daddy. He never brought another woman home that I heard after that. There could have been more that I couldn't hear if they were upstairs or in a different room. I didn't stop to check when I locked him in my room that night. I should have checked! What if I left Emelia behind?"

"Shh," Selina said, glancing over her head at Cal for a moment. "You did the right thing getting out of there. Do you remember where the house was located?"

Mack knew Selina was trying to redirect Bethany before she had a meltdown and couldn't answer more questions. He'd seen it happen with Marlise and Charlotte and didn't want to see it again. The fear was paralyzing for these women after they escaped. Fear that they'd done something wrong. Fear someone was coming after them. Fear that they didn't do enough. That was the hardest part for him to swallow. Watching them so filled with fear that they couldn't even move.

"It was in the woods. Deep in the woods. I ran along the river, and when I came out of the woods, I found a little gas station. I managed to hot-wire an old truck, and on my way out of town, I passed a sign that said Sugarville, Pennsylvania. I made it to a bigger city before I ran out of gas, so I asked The Salvation Army for help. They got me a bus ticket to here."

"Because you heard that Secure One had killed The

Miss?" Charlotte asked, and Bethany nodded her head immediately.

"I heard that Secure One was here when another body was found. I didn't know if you'd still be here, but I didn't know how else to find you."

"That was quick thinking," Mack encouraged the woman. "Why did you want to find us specifically?"

Bethany turned to look at him, and he saw all the fear in her eyes. There was so much that he worried she would drown in it before she finished her story. "If you killed The Miss, then you had to be good people. I needed help and knew I couldn't go to the police."

"Why not?" Charlotte asked with her head tipped in confusion. "The Miss was already dead and The Madame in prison. There was no one left to hurt you."

"But the police might not believe me when I told them my story. I left Little Daddy in that room, and I don't know if he's dead." A shiver ran through her. "If he's not dead, he might find me. If he is dead, the police might be looking for me."

"I can understand that thinking," Charlotte agreed. "How did you get the better of Little Daddy that night?"

"I don't want to talk about that," she whispered so low that Mack almost didn't make out what she said.

"That's okay," Charlotte promised. "You don't have to talk about it, but I need to know if you escaped the same night the body was found here?"

"I think so," Bethany answered. "I ran the first night, was on the bus the second night and here last night."

Bethany was sinking fast, but there was still so much to ask her. Mack was about to ask a question when Charlotte did. "Bethany, you said you were in Pennsylvania when you found the truck, right?"

"Yes, that's what the license plate said. I hope he finds the truck. I don't want to get into trouble for stealing it, but I was so tired and had to get away."

"You won't get in trouble," Cal assured her. "They were extenuating circumstances that the police will understand. Besides, you left it for them to find."

"Do you know how long you ran on foot?" Charlotte asked to complete her question.

"Maybe two hours? I know it was after ten when I left the room and way after midnight when I found the truck."

Mack was making notes on the whiteboard, so he added that to the list. Maybe Mina could do some calculations and get close to the town where Bethany was held hostage.

"You were there a long time, Bethany. I'm impressed that you were strong enough to run that far."

Bethany straightened as though Charlotte's words sparked her determination. "I knew from the beginning that he was going to move me. I spent a couple of months in a stupor but then decided if I was going to try to run when I had the chance, I needed to be strong. He brought me healthy food, and I did a lot of exercise in my room to stay in shape. That was how I overtook him that night. He thought I was asleep, so he dozed off and I took advantage of it."

Cal leaned forward and clasped his hands together casually. "Did you talk to the other women in the house, Bethany?"

"I shared one wall of my bedroom with another room. When I first got there, a woman named Andrea was in that room. Then she left and was replaced by another woman shortly after that. That woman mostly just cried the whole time she was there."

Mack glanced at Charlotte, whose eyes were wide when she looked up at him. He nodded and motioned with his eyes to ask Bethany the next question.

"Did she tell you her name or where she was from?"

"Andrea went to Big Daddy before me. I think I was supposed to be next, and Layla was supposed to be training to go after me."

"Wait, did you say Layla?" Charlotte asked, leaning forward on her chair.

"I think that's what she said her name was, but it was hard to understand because she was always crying, and we had to talk through the wall. I was surprised when Little Daddy said he would take her to Big Daddy before me. He said only he could train her to do what had to be done."

"What had to be done?" Mack asked, shelving the information about Layla for a moment.

"We were being trained to take care of Big Daddy. We had to be ready to do anything he needed from writing a letter to, you know, in bed."

"They had you perform sexual favors? Did you ever see his face?" Cal asked, but Bethany shook her head.

"No. Little Daddy wore a leather mask over his face. I never saw more than his lips and his eyes."

"Do you think you could describe him for me, and I could draw him?" Charlotte asked the woman, whose eyes widened. "If you can't, we all understand."

"I can try," she whispered. "I feel like I failed by running. I didn't get the right information to help you."

"No," Cal said before she finished her sentence. "You didn't fail. You got out alive, and that's miraculous after being there for that long. You survived, Bethany. That's all that matters. Any information you can give us will help, but you did the right thing by running and not looking back."

Bethany nodded as she stared at her hands. "I wish I could have helped the other women, but once you went to Big Daddy, you never came back."

"You've been a huge help to us this morning," Charlotte said, squeezing her hand. "I'm so proud of you for getting out and finding us. We're going to help you now, okay?"

Bethany's face crumpled as she nodded. "I need help. Just like you and Marlise did."

"And we'll get it for you," Selina promised, helping her stand and putting an arm around her.

"We'll take her back to rest," Marlise said to Cal, who nodded. "Then we'll figure out where to go from there for her."

They led the trembling woman from the room, and Mack knew life would never go back to the way it was ten minutes ago.

"Layla was with Big Daddy. Big Daddy has to be The Red River Slayer." Mack heard the fear in Charlotte's voice when she spoke.

"It appears so," said Cal, who sat leaning forward with his hands propped under his chin. "But if Layla had only been dead for three days before we found her, that means Big Daddy kept her for a long time. It's hard to hide a human being for that long."

"Unless they're kept in plain sight," Mack said, lowering the tablet. "Bethany said they had to learn to do everything, including writing a letter. Maybe they're his assistant," he said using quotations, "and they're brainwashed enough not to say otherwise."

"You mean he tells them that they're safe and he will take care of them and give them a job?" Charlotte asked, and Mack nodded. "He had to have convinced Layla she was safe."

"Or that he was on the up and up," Roman agreed.

"You're forgetting that he expects sexual favors," Mina said. "How do you convince someone that is part of an assistant's job?"

Charlotte shrugged and glanced down at her hands. "You give them everything they never had," she whispered. "You buy them nice things, let them get their hair and nails done, tell them you love them. When a woman has never had those things, it's effortless to ply her with them."

Mina started to nod as she spoke and then pointed at her. "She's right. I bet that's how he's doing it. Bethany said they took care of her and brought her healthy food. They wanted the women to be functional when they got to Big Daddy."

"We're still missing a piece of the puzzle," Roman said. He was frustrated by the partial information that didn't make a whole.

"We're missing a lot of the puzzle, Roman," Mack said, his head shaking.

"But wait." Charlotte stood up and grabbed a marker by the whiteboard. She wrote Andrea, Bethany and Layla. "We'll assume, since we don't know, that one of the last five women was Andrea, right?"

Everyone nodded, but Mina spoke. "I'm searching now to see if I can find that name in the databases, but she could have been one of the two that weren't identified, or she hasn't been found yet."

"All of the what-ifs aside," Charlotte said, putting a red *X* through Andrea's name. "We have a pattern developing. Bethany was supposed to go to Big Daddy before Layla, but Little Daddy couldn't train Layla, so she jumped ahead in the queue." She made an arrow over Bethany's name and then put a red *X* through Layla, rewriting Bethany's name on the other side of Layla. "That explains why Bethany was held for so long and why she was being moved to Big Daddy right after we found Layla. However, look what happens when we take Bethany away." She scrubbed out her name with her hand.

"She broke the cycle," Mack said immediately.

Charlotte pointed at him with excitement. "Yes! The woman he was planning to move to the coveted position is gone. So now what? Where does he get his next victim if he has no other women with Little Daddy?"

"And if the cycle is broken, will he stick to his schedule of a death every six weeks, or will he become unpredictable because his perfect order has been broken?" Mack was standing next to Charlotte now by the whiteboard. "Does anyone have an opinion?"

The rest of the team sat open-mouthed as they stared at them. Charlotte was right, the cycle had been broken, and now Mack feared that their perp would react by killing more women.

"He might go underground and try to regroup. Especially if Little Daddy is dead," Roman said. "Or he might have women in other houses that we don't know about yet."

"That I doubt." Mina stood and walked to her computer. "He has to maintain the house where the women are kept with Little Daddy as well as his own living quarters. Unless he's a millionaire, it would be difficult to run three households."

"Then we need to find the guy before he kills another innocent woman," Cal said, his voice tight. "But how? How do we find a guy so good at hiding in plain sight?"

"Do we have a body in the Susquehanna River yet?" Roman asked Charlotte, who stood by the board.

The Susquehanna River was the main river in Pennsylvania and Charlotte knew what he was thinking immediately. "No, but we already know he's transporting these women a long way to leave them in a river, so we can't assume that's the next river."

"We can if the guy's chain of women was broken," Mack said. "It would be safe to assume that he'll act rashly now. Either he's going to kill a random woman, or he's going to go underground, and it will be another two years before we hear from him again. We don't want that."

"We need to go to Pennsylvania," Roman said.

Cal shook his head. "Impossible. I don't have the staffing for that. We're already stretched too thin."

"I have Efren coming on, but he can't be here until tomorrow," Mina piped up from behind her computer. "Then we have the party security to worry about next."

Mack met Charlotte's gaze across the board and knew what she was thinking. She was going to figure out a way to get to Pennsylvania and offer herself up for The Red River Slayer to grab. He wasn't going to let that happen.

Chapter Fifteen

Marlise and Selina arrived to fill them in on Bethany's condition. "She needs medical care," Selina said, "but I can't convince her to leave yet. I keep telling her she needs to talk to the police, but she's afraid to do that too. She has been held in captivity for years. She needs a psychiatrist and a therapist to help her."

"We agree," Cal said. "But we can give her one more day before we force anything on her."

Charlotte was trying to follow the conversation and sort out the information in her head and on the board. Thirty-three senators were running for reelection, but so far, only six, possibly eight, bodies had been found.

"There's no way," Charlotte muttered as she stared at the board. "There's just no way."

Mack walked up to her and took her shoulder. "There's no way for what, sweetheart?"

"For this guy to kill the number of women necessary to equal the thirty-three senators running for reelection. Now that we know he keeps them for an extended period, if Bethany's captor is The Red River Slayer, there isn't enough time." Charlotte looked over at Mina. "Did they do autopsies on all the women?" Mina nodded immediately. "Did they get a time of death on all of them?"

"No," Mina said, standing and walking around the computer. "Layla's was the first autopsy that was within that tight of a window. It was impossible to know with the other women."

"You're saying they could have been dead much longer?" Mack asked.

"Whether they took that long to float to shore or he held them after death, there's no way to know. It could be pure coincidence that the women were found at that time interval."

"My science teacher said that rivers don't freeze over like lakes," Ella said from the back of the room. Charlotte had forgotten she was there since she'd had her earphones in and was watching a movie. "But shallow parts of rivers can freeze. If a body floated under the ice and got trapped, it wouldn't move again until spring arrived. He also said that the streamflow of rivers changes by seasons."

"Following that train of thought," Mina said, standing up. "If spring hits and there's more snowmelt in one area of the river, that pushes a big deluge of water through the river at a high rate of speed."

"Which could easily upend a body trapped in sludge," Mack finished.

"If he's trying to make a point, wouldn't he want the bodies to be found immediately? He's taking a chance they won't be found where he wanted them to be or at all."

"Serial killers don't think the same as we do, Mack," Mina said, and Charlotte smiled. Mina was going to school him about the psychology of psychopaths, and she couldn't wait. "They do things that aren't logical to us, but to them, it's completely logical. Sometimes, they don't care if and when their victims are found."

"That would explain the longer period with no bodies," Roman added.

"You're saying we got lucky finding Layla just three days after her death." Mack waited for someone to answer.

"Highly probable," Mina confirmed. "This is spring, and the river is high and swift. He may have misjudged how long it would take her to come ashore this time."

Charlotte glanced over at Ella, who was staring at the list of names on the whiteboard. "Did I forget one?" she asked the teen, who shook her head.

"No. The names are all there. Your comment about there being no way for him to kill that many women started me thinking." She took a marker from the board and put checkmarks next to nine names.

"What do the checkmarks mean?" Charlotte asked.

"Those nine senators are committee members on fisheries, wildlife and water. I know because my dad is on the committee."

Charlotte noticed the surprise on Mack's face even before he spoke. "Would this committee deal with rivers?"

Ella shrugged. "Well, sure. I know there's a big fight about dams and the damage they do to the waterways. Or something like that anyway. My dad talks about it all the time."

Mack grabbed a marker and underlined the nine senators' names on their states. There were three senators' states that had rivers where bodies were found, which included Senator Dorian. "If I'm following this correctly, the three bodies recently found match up to a state with a senator on this list."

"And that means instead of twenty-seven more women, there could be six more before this is over," Charlotte said, her voice filled with fury and fear. "We can't let that happen."

Mack walked over to Mina and leaned on her desk. "Can you see if the previous reelection cycle river deaths match the states of any previous committee members?"

"I'm on it," she said, putting her hands on the keyboard. "Give me thirty minutes."

"If this is some nut trying to bring attention to a cause by killing women, we need to stop him now," Mack said, walking back to Charlotte and putting a protective hand on her back.

Cal stood. "I couldn't agree more. Charlotte, take Ella back to her room, please. Eric, Roman and Mack, you're with me. We'll reconvene here in thirty."

Charlotte put her arm around Ella and walked with her to the kitchen. "Forget going to your room. We're going to have breakfast, and then you'll be there to hear what Mina discovered."

"I don't know if Cal will like that," Ella said, nervously chewing on her lip.

"Too bad. If it weren't for you picking up on that pattern, we'd still be stuck in neutral. A good friend recently told me we must control our power if we want respect. This is us demanding respect."

She winked at the young girl and then led her through the kitchen door for pancakes and juice.

HE LISTENED TO the incessant ringing in his ear as he sat at his desk, the low drone of voices outside his office door reminding him to play it cool. The call went to voice mail again, and he angrily slammed the phone down on his blotter. So much for playing it cool.

"Where the hell is he?" His growl scared the cat, who darted back under the leather sofa against one wall. It was his ex-wife's cat, but she'd decided she hadn't wanted it when she moved to the Bahamas to live with her new boyfriend. He often wondered if they were enjoying their extended time under the blue-green waters.

A smile lifted his lips at the thought. That memory didn't solve his problem though. He had no idea where his guy was or why he wasn't answering his phone. Maybe he was just busy, but even he couldn't swallow that excuse anymore. If that were the case, he would have called him back after the first ten voice mails, each one increasingly angrier.

He glanced at the clock and sighed. He was going to have to mix business with pleasure. He already regretted what was to come, but his guy had left him no choice. He walked to a side door of his office and opened it. "Miss Andrea, I'd like to see you for a moment."

He waited while the young blond woman joined him in the office. Today she was wearing a pencil skirt that accentuated her bottom and a silk blouse that made her look professional and sex kitten at the same time. He motioned for her to close the door, and she couldn't hide the apprehension on her face as she turned to do it. His desire stirred. She knew what was to come and would obey him no matter what he asked her.

When she turned back, her face changed to that of a contented woman ready to please her protector. "How can I help?"

She asked the question that made his beast roar to life, but he forced it down. This was not the time or the place.

"Have you enjoyed your time with me, Miss Andrea?"

He propped his elbows on his sizeable executive desk and steepled his fingers against his lips.

"Very much so," she agreed. She sat in the chair he motioned to and crossed her legs. "I'm quite happy working for you."

His mouth watered at the sight of her tanned skin just waiting for his touch, but he didn't. Touch, that is. "And I'm happy to hear you say that, Andrea. I need a favor, and I can't ask anyone else. No one can know about this."

"I wouldn't tell a soul." She batted her lashes at him the way he demanded of her, but he wasn't looking to score today…at least not yet.

"Good. Be ready to leave in thirty minutes."

"We're taking a trip? Is it for work or pleasure?"

"A little of both, Miss Andrea. A little of both," he said, allowing his inner beast to come through in the smile he offered her. "Work first with pleasure to follow."

She stood and left his office, his gaze savoring the moment. It would be the last time he'd see that bottom walking out his door.

Chapter Sixteen

"A macabre scene played out on the bank of the Susque-hanna River this morning," the newscaster began, and Charlotte swiveled toward the television in the corner of the room. "There were two bodies discovered by a fish-erman in a weed-filled slough this morning. Initially, the police suspected The Red River Slayer had killed again until they discovered the bodies were locked in a lovers' embrace. The man and woman were taken to the local medical examiner's office to await identification. If you think you may have information about this couple, please call—"

Charlotte didn't hear another word as she was already out the door and running to command central. Eric was alone in the room, staring at the whiteboard when she arrived.

"Eric," she said, out of breath enough that she needed to pause before saying anything more. "Two bodies were found in Pennsylvania this morning along the river."

He whirled around before she finished speaking. "Women?"

"That's the weird part," she said, walking into the room. "They said it was a man and a woman locked in a lovers' embrace."

"Did they give any other information?" he asked, grabbing a walkie from the table.

"They were taken to the local medical examiner for identification."

"Secure two, Echo," he said into the black box.

"Secure one, Whiskey," came Mina's voice.

"Mina, can you come to the office? I need some help on the computer."

"Be there in two," she answered, and then the box went silent.

"It has to be a coincidence." Eric was addressing Charlotte this time. "Other than the river, it's too far off the norm for our perp. There would be no reason for him to kill a man."

"Unless it was Little Daddy."

"How does the woman come into play then?"

"I don't know, okay! I'm just telling you what the news report said." Frustrated, Charlotte plopped down in a chair and rubbed her face with her hands. She needed sleep, but she suspected that wasn't happening soon.

Mina jogged into the room, and Eric explained what he needed. She started searching for the early copies of the story to see if one had more information than the other. While she did that, Charlotte paced. She had too much nervous energy. Eric might not believe her, but she had a gut feeling about this guy, and her gut never lied. How the woman came into play, she didn't know yet, but if anyone could figure it out, Mina could. They'd have to tell Cal what they discovered when he landed back at Secure One. He'd taken Roman and Marlise back with him, so the team at headquarters wasn't shorthanded. Mina stayed behind to help with anything computer-based since she could work remotely for Secure One simultaneously. Charlotte was suddenly glad she'd stayed.

"From what I can gather, a fisherman found the couple early this morning. The police reported that it was difficult to disengage the pair, but once they did, they realized the couple had died together."

"Rigor mortis?" Eric asked.

"Seems like it," Mina said from behind the computer.

"If rigor was set, then they had to have died recently. Full rigor only lasts for twenty-four hours after death. If the water was cold though, rigor could last much longer." Eric put his hand on his hip. "Anything else?"

"No, they don't have much to go on right now. The police asked the public to come forward with any information."

"Where did they find the bodies?" Charlotte asked. "Near a town?"

"Every station reported it, so I can't use that as the first identifier. I might have to go through some back doors to find that information."

"They worked hard to keep the location from the news report," Eric said, pacing toward the door. "They didn't say where the bodies were found or what ME has them."

"Let me look into this," Mina said as she typed. "If I can come up with the ME who has the bodies, or a report entered by a police station, I'll know within a few miles where they were found."

Charlotte grabbed a walkie and held it up. "Call me when you know something. I'm going to offer breaks."

Eric waved her off, and she headed for the stairs where Mack was standing guard over the women. Selina had stayed back to take care of Bethany until she could transfer her to a facility, and Ella was doing schoolwork in her room. Charlotte knew Mack didn't need a break, but she wanted to update him.

You want to see him.

With an eye roll, Charlotte shut that voice down. There was no sense even considering a life with Mack. He might want her at the moment, but there was a lifetime of things he didn't know about her.

And he doesn't care.

The grunt she gave that voice was loud and clear as she stomped up the stairs.

Do the things that make you feel powerful, even if that means you have to take those things back from the toxic people too.

Mina's words ran through her mind as she hit the landing and headed toward the bedrooms. What made her feel powerful? That was the question she had to answer.

STANDING AROUND DOING nothing was making Mack antsy. He needed to move, but there was nowhere to go. His gut told him something was about to go down, and he widened his stance a bit in acknowledgment. When Cal returned to Secure One, he would immediately send in the extra help he'd hired for the campaign party rather than wait. Once Mina's new guy arrived, Mack would hand over the bodyguard duties with gratitude. There was nothing Mack hated more than standing around idle.

He ran a hand over his face and closed his eyes for a moment. Exhaustion hung on him after the night he'd had, but he could only blame himself. Instead of dreaming about Charlotte, he should have reminded himself that he couldn't get involved with her. That reminder had nothing to do with who she was and everything to do with what she'd been through in life. She didn't need his ugly baggage to carry when she had enough of her own—

"Kiss me."

Mack looked down at the woman standing in his path with confusion. "What?"

"I said, kiss me."

"I heard what you said," he whispered, leaning closer. "I'm confused why you said it."

"You said you wouldn't kiss me again until I asked you to. I just asked. Now kiss me."

Mack lifted a brow. He liked her spunk, but this felt like a test he could fail no matter his choice. "I would love to, but there are cameras everywhere. We should save that for a time when we're—"

Finishing the sentence wasn't an option when she grabbed him and planted her lips on his. Hers were warm and tasted of sweet strawberries. His head swam at the sensations she evoked in him until he was left little choice but to grasp her waist and pull her to him. He shouldn't be kissing her, but none of him cared. If Charlotte was initiating a kiss, he would enjoy every moment of it, in case it was the only one he ever got.

Tilting his head, he dug in deeper, still letting her control it, but pushing back enough for her to know he was all in no matter where she took it. He wouldn't force it further than she was comfortable with, but he would need the strength of a god to let her go when she ended it. The little moan that escaped the back of her throat fanned his desire until he was sure their closeness revealed his true feelings for her. Again, not one part of him cared. It wasn't a secret that he desired her, and this kiss made it known that she felt the same, even if the whole situation was complicated beyond measure.

Her tongue traced the closed split in his lips until he parted them and let her roam his mouth, his tongue tangling with hers until neither one could breathe, and they had to fall apart just to suck in air. She stood before him, her chest heaving as she lowered her forehead to his chest.

"I shouldn't have done that. I'm sorry."

Mack tipped her chin up until they made eye contact. "Do. Not. Apologize. In case you didn't notice, I loved every second of it, so no apology is needed."

"But the cameras—"

"Will show them what they already know," he said with a wink. "I am curious to hear what changed between last night and today."

"Mina told me to do what makes me feel powerful, even if I have to take those things back from my toxic past."

"That's good advice," he agreed, tucking a piece of hair behind her ear as she rested her forehead on his chest. "Being the one to initiate the kiss took back your power from the men who always said they owned you, right?" Her head nodded against his sweater, but she still didn't look up. Rather than push her away and force eye contact that would make her uncomfortable, Mack wrapped his arms around her and squeezed. "I'm proud of you. It's not easy to leave our bad experiences in the past and live in the moment. Thank you for letting me be the one to help you do that."

"I didn't use you, Mack. I wanted to kiss you." She finally lifted her face to his and smiled.

"I know you didn't use me, Char. That wasn't what I was implying. I was genuinely thanking you for trusting me enough to know you could. For the record, I wanted to kiss you too. I think I proved that last night."

Her head bob was enough to tell him he'd gotten through to her, and she understood. Slowly, he loosened his arms so she could step back and collect herself. He figured Mina was in command central doing a fist pump if she'd seen them on camera, and he couldn't stop the smirk that filled his face. Until he remembered Eric was down there too.

Mack wasn't sure what was up with Eric, but something was. He was constantly defensive and pushing back on any order Mack or Cal gave. They'd been friends for a dozen years, so he hoped if Eric had a real problem, he'd come to them and talk openly about it, but so far, that hadn't happened. Mack made a mental note to talk to Cal about it once he was back at Secure One and had a moment to think.

"I also have an update to give you," Charlotte said after straightening her hair. Mack listened while she filled him in on the two bodies found in Pennsylvania.

"That's odd, but not necessarily tied to The Red River Slayer."

Charlotte shrugged when she nodded. "I know, but they were found in the same river as the one Bethany was near when she ran." She held her hand out at the door on his right. "She did say she wasn't sure if she killed the guy."

Mack considered this but then shook his head. "It still doesn't make sense. If she killed him, he wouldn't end up in the river. He would have decayed in the house."

"You're ignoring the obvious, Mack. Big Daddy."

"You think Big Daddy found Little Daddy and threw him in the river? Who's the woman?"

A text alert came in, and Mack grabbed his phone. There

was a text from Mina, and all it said was get a room. He couldn't hide the smirk on his face, and Charlotte noticed.

"What? Is it Cal?"

He turned the phone for her to read. Her lips tipped up, and she bit the inside of her cheek to keep from laughing. "I'm not great at stealth mode yet."

Mack's laughter filled the hallway, and he put his arm around her shoulders and brushed his lips across her ear. "I'm not complaining."

Her huff was easy to decipher and only made his smirk grow into a full-blown grin. Char had no idea how special she was to him. "Back to the case," she said in the perfunctory tone of an experienced teacher. "The woman."

"Oh, yes, the woman. It doesn't fit, Char."

Her finger came up into his chest. "Maybe not, but you were the one who said removing Bethany from the chain may make him do something rash or unexpected."

"Fair point," he agreed. "I did say that, and this would be rash and unexpected. Hopefully, Mina has something for us by the time Cal gets back to Secure One. Then we can set up a conference call with him to discuss it."

"We need to go to Pennsylvania, Mack."

Her statement was so decisive that he paused on his next thought. "We? Whatever for?"

"I don't know, but my gut tells me we'll find pieces of the puzzle out there."

Mack grasped her shoulders and held her gaze. "This isn't our puzzle to solve. If the feds got wind that we were sticking our nose into this case again, they might lock Cal down, and I don't want that to happen."

"Neither do I, but they aren't doing their job!" she exclaimed in frustration. "They should have solved this case already!"

Mack didn't react to her frustration except to squeeze her shoulder as a reminder that he was there. Once she settled, he spoke gently to her. "I understand you're angry about this case, and you've come by that right naturally. I can separate myself from the case more because I didn't live that kind of life. Then I think about you, and I know in my heart that it could have been you if you'd played the wrong card at the wrong time. The feds may not devote time to this case because the victims are women without families. They don't feel as compelled to solve it quickly since no one is prodding them to keep after it."

"Yes," she said, her shoulders loosening in his grasp. "No one understands that part of it. It could have been me, and I don't want it to be another woman I know. I can't let that happen, Mack."

He nodded with her just to give her a moment to own those feelings of fear and determination. "Okay, let's see what Mina finds, and then we'll talk to Cal about letting us do more boots-on-the-ground work in Pennsylvania. Our turnaround will be quick though, since the party is in ten days, and it all rests on Efren getting here to help out."

"Understood," she agreed with a nod.

Mack couldn't help but wonder if her intuition was correct. If their perp found Little Daddy dead and Bethany gone, would he kill a random woman just to make a point? If Mina's answer to that question was yes, then he wouldn't ask Cal if they could go to Pennsylvania—he'd tell him they were going.

Chapter Seventeen

The two-hour ride was made light by the occasional country road he'd pull over on to be assisted by his assistant. It was a perk none of his colleagues had, but none of them were nearly as brilliant as they thought they were. No one suspected a thing, but he wasn't surprised by that. As someone who studied the human mind, he'd learned that a simple explanation was enough for 99 percent of the population. Thankfully, his interactions with the 1 percent of the population that asked too many questions were few and far between. When he ran across one, he usually had to remove them from the population rather unexpectedly.

He put the car in Park and stared straight ahead. He hated what he was about to do, but there was no choice. It had been four days since he'd had contact with his wingman, and he was worried. Dead was okay. Arrested was not.

"Where are we? There's like, no one out here."

He opened his door and walked around the car to open her door and help her out. He was a gentleman after all. "This is a friend's house," he lied. "I haven't been able to reach him, and I thought someone should check on him."

"The police are closer than a two-hour drive," she pointed out. "They could have done a welfare check."

Shame, he thought. She had been in the 99 percent,

but she just landed herself in the 1 percent. Honestly, he was surprised. He had her pegged for the typical bimbo. After all, she'd been doing his bidding without question for months. Today, she decided to question him. It didn't matter, she wasn't coming home with him anyway, but it was a reminder that he would have to make it clearer to his next assistant never to question him.

He unlocked the door and motioned her through before him. "Wow, you have a key to his house. Are you that close to him?"

"You should ask fewer questions," he said as he walked through the empty house.

"Is he moving? There's no furniture in here."

The man's sigh echoed through the cavernous space. Suddenly, she was *Chatty Cathy*. He rolled his eyes and flipped on the light to the basement, waiting for her to meet him there. When she did, he motioned for her to go down the stairs, but a flash of self-preservation struck. If his guy was down there, and she saw him, she might try to run. He couldn't be chasing her through the woods if he had a job to clean up here. Without a second thought, he shoved her from behind, and she sailed through the air and landed with a thud at the bottom.

He strolled down the stairs and smiled down at her. "Don't go anywhere. I'll be right back."

He stepped over her twisted body and noticed the door at the end of the hall was closed. That was either a good thing or a very bad thing. He dug out the key and stuck it in the lock with a sigh. He had a bad feeling about this, but he pushed the door in and flipped on the light. What he saw was too much to comprehend, and his beast broke free and took over. All he could do was stand there and watch.

CHARLOTTE WAS FIXING Mack and Selina lunch when Mina walked into the kitchen. The man she had with her held himself in a manner that said messing with him was bad for your health.

"Everyone, meet Efren Brenna."

Efren shook hands with everyone while wearing an easy smile. "Thanks for the welcome. I know these are unusual circumstances, but Mina and I go way back. You can trust me to get the job done."

"I could have guarded the women," Selina muttered around the last of her sandwich, and Charlotte lifted a brow but didn't say anything.

"You could have, but we need you to care for Bethany, not worry about her and Ella."

"I have a lot of experience guarding VIPs. I'll take care of the senator's daughter," Efren said, offering Selina a calm smile, but stiffness to his shoulders told Charlotte he was on the defense.

"Aren't we lucky then?" Selina said with an even tighter smile. "I better head back up and do vitals on Bethany. Physically, she's fine, but emotionally and mentally, she needs a facility. When will I be able to transfer her and get the hell out of here?"

Charlotte glanced at Mina, who had also picked up on Selina's catty attitude. Something was up because Selina was never contrary, and you could always depend on her.

"Once Efren is upstairs to replace Eric, I have some updates to share with the team. We may have a question or two to ask her, but it will be safe to find her the help she needs after that."

"Any questions go through me," Selina said, poking herself in the chest while she eyed Efren up and down with disdain. "Call me on the walkie, and I'll ask her. I'm not putting her through another Q and A like this morning."

"That would be fine." Mina's tone of voice was calm and accepting, but Charlotte knew she too was wondering what was going on with their friend. Maybe it was just this place. Everyone was walking on eggshells, wondering when the next body would show up.

Selina glared at Efren before she left the room, and they all looked at each other for a few moments before anyone spoke. "What's wrong with her?" Mack asked. "I don't think I've ever heard her speak to anyone that way."

"Same," Mina said, still staring after their friend. "Maybe this case is getting to her. She's the one who keeps patching these women up." Mina turned to Charlotte. "No offense meant."

"None taken, you're correct. It's got to be hard on Selina. We need this to end. Do you have updates on the last two bodies found?"

"Yes!" Mina said, clapping her hands together. "Let me take Efren up to meet Eric and take over guarding Ella. Then we can all meet to discuss the new information."

"We'll meet you in the office in five minutes," Mack said, carrying his plate to the sink. "Glad to have you on the team, Efren, despite the lack of welcome from some of our members."

"No offense taken," Efren assured them. "I know what it's like to walk into an established team. You have to find your place on it and then earn your stripes. I've done it before, and I can do it again if this assignment is long-term. For now, I'll take care of Ella and help with the party."

He shook Mack's hand again and then left the kitchen behind Mina. Charlotte was about to start cleaning up the dishes, but Mack grasped her elbow to stop her. "Leave them. We have a few minutes, and we need to discuss something."

"Mack, I won't demand that you kiss me again if that's what you're worrie—"

Before she could finish, his lips crashed down on hers and stole her breath away. She could feel the tremble of desire go through him when she opened her mouth and let him in. She planted her hands on his chest to push him away, but with his strong muscles rippling under her hands and his tongue in her mouth, she didn't want to push him away. The thought made her body tingle with heat and desire in a way it never had before. The therapist had tried to help her understand that there was a difference between being with a man she wanted to be with versus being with a man she was forced to be with, but she struggled to understand it until this very moment. Suddenly, she understood that a man who cared would kiss her differently than a man who wanted to take advantage of her.

Charlotte leaned into his chest and sighed. She felt safe with Mack. After all the men she'd had to deal with working for The Madame and The Miss, she never thought she'd feel safe with a man. Especially a man the size and strength of Mack Holbock, but somehow, he had worked himself around her defenses to show her the difference. With the other men, her heart pounded with fear and dread. With Mack, it pounded with want and maybe a little hope that she wasn't too damaged to love someone else.

The kiss ended, but Mack returned twice more for a quick kiss of her lips before he released her for good. "To be clear," he said, with his breath heavy in his chest. "You never have to demand anything from me. I give it to you freely. Understood?"

"You're as clear as water," she whispered, her fingers going to her lips to check if they were still there. The man could kiss, and the heat kicked up fast and furious when he took over her lips. "If that wasn't what you wanted to talk about, what was it?"

Mack motioned for her to sit and leaned in close to her ear. "Are we a team, Char?" Her nod was immediate. "Are you ready to prove it?" He gazed at her with a brow up and waited for her answer. She nodded once, and he grinned as he took her hand. "Then let's go prove it."

AFTER THEY MET with Mina and the rest of the team at lunch, they'd immediately hopped on a flight from Minneapolis to Chicago and from there to Harrisburg, Pennsylvania. Charlotte hadn't asked how Mina managed to get them on flights so quickly because she suspected it wasn't the same way others did. Once they landed in Harrisburg, she had a rental car waiting for them too. Mina was good at her job, but now they had to step up and do the rest.

Mack put the rental car into Park and pulled out his phone. "Mina got us the only room she could find this far out in the sticks. As she put it," he added, glancing at her. They'd been traveling for well over six hours, and she was ready to stretch her legs.

"As long as there's a shower, I don't even care if it's the Bates Motel," she said, bringing a smile to his face.

He chuckled and motioned for her to wait while he grabbed their bags from the back seat and helped her out of the car. They walked toward the small motel to check in, and Charlotte couldn't help but hesitate.

"Everything's okay," Mack promised, putting a protective arm around her waist. "No one is going to hurt you."

"It's not that. It's just the last time I was at one of these motels, it was rent-by-the-hour." She paused and then shook her head. "Never mind."

Mack cocked his head, but before he could say anything, they were at the small check-in area of the motel. There was an empty chair but a light in the room behind it. "Hello? Anyone around?"

A man popped his head out and held up his finger. When he finally came out, he was wearing nothing but a pair of shorts and a tank top. "Sorry about that. You woke me from my beauty sleep. What can I do for you?"

"I'm Mack Holbock. There should be a reservation for us."

"Oh, yes, I only have one room left though. The woman who called didn't think you'd mind."

"No problem at all. We won't be here long."

Charlotte bit her lip to keep from groaning at his choice of words. As though things weren't awkward enough between them, now the man thought she and Mack were getting a room for their secret tryst.

After they had the keys and found the room, Mack opened the door and motioned her in. When he flipped on the light, she was glad he couldn't see the grimace on her face. There was one queen bed in the middle of the room and nothing else. Mack would fill most of that bed by himself. She couldn't imagine having to be that close to him all night and not touch him.

"I'll take the chair. You can have the bed," Mack whispered as he moved around her to set their bags down.

She eyed the chair, and there was no way he would fit

in it, much less sleep in it. "We're adults, Mack. We can share the bed."

"Fine with me if it's fine with you," he said so casually that it felt wrong. "Do you want to shower first, or should I?"

"I'll go." She grabbed her bag and disappeared behind the bathroom door to escape the awkward situation. The shower was hot, but she finished quickly so there was enough hot water left for him. After dressing in her pants and T-shirt, she left the bathroom. "Next."

He gave her a tight smile as he walked around her and disappeared behind the door. She set her bag down on the floor and eyed the small desk he'd already covered with technical equipment from Secure One. She hoped he didn't plan to have another virtual meeting with the team tonight. She wasn't sure she would stay awake for it.

When they'd all met in the office after lunch, Mina had a plethora of information. The couple was found on the riverbank near Southwood, Pennsylvania. When they put that into their map and asked for directions to Sugarville, the town Bethany had stopped at, it was less than an hour's drive away. It made sense that Bethany was probably held somewhere in the same area where the bodies were found. It was sloppy on the part of the killer if that were the case, but if he had bodies to clean up, he might not have had a choice.

It wasn't until they discovered that Senator Tanner from Pennsylvania was not only up for reelection but also on the subcommittee that Cal agreed they needed boots on the ground. If this was The Red River Slayer, he was coming unglued, and the possibility of finding another body in the area was high. He still hadn't hit five other committee members' home states, but they were all on the East Coast. However, Cal didn't think he would stick with his original plan. If the killer felt threatened, he'd go underground just like he had last time. He'd have had to get rid of the two bodies, assuming the man was Little Daddy, but he would likely be highly cautious for some time now.

All they needed was a little time and a break to lead them to the house where Bethany was kept. Charlotte didn't know for sure, but her gut told her the man found in the river today was Little Daddy. They didn't know the identities of either person, but Mina was going to keep them abreast of any updates as they came in. In the meantime, she and Mack would use a grid-like search of the area to find the house. It was a long shot, and they didn't have much time, but they couldn't sit around and do nothing.

Cal was afraid Bethany wouldn't be safe until The Red River Slayer was found. It was a thought that hadn't entered her mind, but he was right. Since they didn't know who he was, they couldn't protect her if she wasn't with them. Selina wasn't happy about the delay in transferring her care and made it known, which was highly unusual. It was a rare occasion when someone questioned Cal's authority, but Selina kept pushing the yard line until he agreed to bring a therapist in to meet with Bethany. Selina still left the meeting with a huff, and Charlotte was worried there was something more going on with her.

For right now though, she didn't have time to worry about anything but locating The Red River Slayer. Women everywhere were in danger and weren't even aware of it. They could be snatched off the street by this sicko and never be seen again until they floated to shore. Charlotte wouldn't let that happen. She was here with Mack not only to prove herself to Cal and the team but to herself. Cal wanted to send Eric instead of her, but Mack insisted he needed a woman with him to soften their questioning. When Cal finally agreed, she was sure Eric gave her a death glare. Something was up with the Secure One team, and she hoped they'd be able to pull off the senator's campaign party without showing dissent in the ranks. If anything happened at that party to endanger a sitting senator or their family, there would be hell to pay, and it would be Cal's head on the chopping block. She and Mack were needed in Minnesota, so time was of the essence. She just hoped when they returned to the state, it wasn't in a body bag.

Chapter Eighteen

The shifting of the woman on top of him was torture. Mack had to figure out a way to slide her back down onto the bed and off his chest before she woke up from the hard rod poking her in the belly. He'd seen the look on her face when she saw the one bed in the room, and it was easy to imagine what she was thinking. He never wanted Char to feel like he didn't respect her or her body. He did, and he'd bend over backward to prove it, even if that meant standing in the corner to sleep. At least the corner gave him better odds of getting shut-eye than being in bed with her on top of him. Her soft, sweet body warmed his skin, and he wanted to let his hands roam over her back and waist to cup her tight backside. He'd dreamed about touching her that way for months, but he wouldn't. She wasn't ready for that kind of relationship yet.

She's not ready, or you're not ready?

Mack tried not to groan at the voice just as she murmured his name.

"Why are you sleeping with a gun?"

He grunted with unabashed amusement. "Sweetheart, that's not my gun. I'm just happy to see you."

The warmth he'd cherished disappeared when she sat up in bed to rub her face.

"In my defense, you were on top of me when I woke up. I wanted to move you but didn't want to wake you."

"What time is it?"

"Only three a.m. Go back to sleep."

"As though that's going to happen," she muttered. She scooted closer to the edge of the bed. "I'm sorry for," she waved her hand over his groin, "that. It wasn't intentional."

"I know," he promised. He patiently rubbed Char's back while she gathered her thoughts. "You were scared and needed someone, which is why I climbed into bed and didn't sleep in the chair."

"I'm not scared of you, Mack," she said, crossing her arms over her chest, but he noticed she didn't ask him to remove his hand.

"I didn't say of me, but I saw the look on your face when we approached the building tonight. You were scared."

"The last time I was in a place like this, I was forced to do things to *earn my keep*, as The Miss used to say. Those men saw me as nothing more than a way to scratch an itch or to have control over someone smaller than them."

He paused. "I bet Mina didn't think about it when she booked the room. I'm sorry. We should have been more considerate."

Her blond hair swayed across her back when she shook her head and it brushed over his already hyperaware skin. "Don't worry about it. There wasn't much choice if we wanted to sleep for the night. Not that we're getting much sleep."

"Hey," Mack said, sitting up and wrapping his arm around her side to pull her into him. "Take a moment to feel your feelings, okay? I know you're trying to take your power back, but sometimes you have to acknowledge the past and how it shaped you. Some experiences in life leave scars on our minds. When that happens, we'll always struggle in that situation. It's understandable, and I accept you no matter what, Char."

Slowly, her head lowered to his shoulder, and she sighed. "You're talking about PTSD."

"I suppose I am. I don't know many who have fought battles in war who don't have it in one form or another."

"Maybe for soldiers, but I wasn't a soldier."

"Oh, darling, you absolutely were," he whispered, resting his cheek on her head. "You lived through those battles, but just like mine, they left scars. My battles were more straightforward. I knew my enemy, and I had a lethal weapon to defend myself. You had neither of those things. All you had were your wits and a prayer."

"My wits kept me alive, but the prayers didn't work," she murmured, burrowing her head into his chest.

"You'll never have to use your wits with me. I'll never tell you to let it go or get over it. I'm a safe zone for you to feel what you need to feel, Char."

When she laughed, there was no humor behind it. "But you aren't safe, Mack," she whispered. "When we're together, the things I feel are confusing. When you kiss me, there's so much emotion in my chest that I don't know what to do with it."

"Confusing good or confusing bad?"

"Good, but also bad. I like how you make me feel, and I like being with you, but I also know you deserve someone who hasn't fought battles while unarmed and outmanned."

Mack kissed the top of her head. He wanted to connect with her again, if only briefly. "Life doesn't work that way, Char. I will live with my disability for the rest of my life.

What if I said you deserve better than being with someone who can't walk without strapping on braces every morning? Would you agree and walk away?"

"Of course not." Her eyes sparked with anger as she sat up to glare at him. "The scars on your legs don't make you less than anyone else. They're just part of you."

"More proof that life doesn't work that way. When we connect with another soul, that's all that matters."

Char was silent for so long he thought she'd fallen asleep as he rubbed her back. "Do you think our souls have connected?" she whispered. "Like, do you think soulmates exist?"

"Do soulmates exist? Yes. I only have to look at Cal and Marlise. Did our souls connect?" he asked, running a finger down her cheek. "The moment I took you in my arms."

"Mack, will you show me what you mean? I learn better that way."

When he gazed into her eyes, the truth was obvious. She wanted him to show her the connection. He scooted backward on the bed until he could lean against the headboard and then pulled her onto his lap to straddle him. "If you get uncomfortable or scared, tell me to stop."

Her only response was to capture his lips and press herself against his chest. She wrapped her arms around his neck and buried her fingers in his hair. He held her around the waist, her warmth a balm to his injured soul while he searched for a foothold on this slippery slope. He was afraid he'd fall over the edge and do something he shouldn't. But her kisses and caresses made him want more. They made him want to be more for her even when she didn't ask. He still wanted to give her everything.

The need for air overtook his desire to keep caressing her tongue. He let his lips fall away from hers to trail down her neck to her collarbone. He suckled gently, raising goose bumps on her flesh as he made love to her with his lips. He tugged her T-shirt lower to kiss the tender skin at the base of her neck. Her pulse raced beneath his lips because of him. For him. With him.

"Mack," she moaned, the sound of his name airy on her lips. "I want more." To make her point, she rubbed her hips against his desire, dragging a moan from him.

He didn't want to hurt her. He also didn't know if he could make love to her and walk away when the inevitable happened. The old saying about it better to have loved and lost came back to him, and he suckled hard on her chest, leaving his mark where only she would see.

While she was lost in the sensation of his lips, he slid his hand under her shirt. His fingertips skirted across her ribs to the edge of her breast. She stilled, so he did too, waiting for her to decide what she wanted.

"I want you, Mack, but I don't know if I can do it. I want to, but I can't promise—"

With his finger to her lips, he hushed her. "I understand, sweetheart. You don't have to do anything. That's not why we're here tonight. I'm safe. I won't take more than you can give. You're in control of everything."

It was as though she needed to hear him validate her fears and desire in a way that put her in control. He saw the shift in her when she remembered that she could trust him to stop if she said stop. And he would, even if it killed him to hold her until she fell asleep and nothing else. He would. He would protect her, whether on the job or in his bed.

Before he could clear his head of the thoughts running through it, Charlotte lowered her lips again and drank from his, her desire no longer capped by fear but fanned by trust.

Trust.

The word hit him in the gut as she leaned back and stripped her T-shirt off, revealing her perfectly taut nipples waiting for his attention. He took a few moments to appreciate her beauty and learn her curves, picturing the path his tongue would take from her nipple to her navel and then if she was ready, lower still. "You are gorgeous," he whispered, his finger trailing down her ribs. "I want all of you, Char."

"Even the broken parts?" she asked in a whisper that made his chest clench from an emotion he didn't want to acknowledge.

"Especially the broken parts."

Then her lips were back on his, and he knew, given enough time and trust, they'd heal each other.

"SECURE TWO, WHISKEY." Mina's voice filled the room, and Mack scrambled to answer before she hung up.

"Secure one, Mike."

The tablet came to life, and Mina's face filled the screen. "Good morning, early birds," she said, her trained eye taking in Charlotte on the bed as she tied on her shoes. It was the reason she insisted on making the bed rather than leaving the bedclothes rumpled.

"Good morning, Mina. Do you have an update?" Mack asked. "We were just making a plan of attack."

"Glad I caught you then," she said, typing on her computer as she spoke. Charlotte was always in awe of how she could do both and not lose track of either. "I have an identity on the man found in the river yesterday."

"Seriously?" Charlotte stood up and walked closer to the tablet. "That was fast."

"Fast, but not helpful. His name is Chip Winston."

"Did you run specs on him?" Mack asked, strapping on his gun belt and vest.

"I did, but lo and behold, he doesn't exist except on paper."

"Washed?" Charlotte asked with surprise. "How is that possible?"

"I don't know, but I'm still digging. Someone washed him, but I don't believe he was CIA or FBI. I can't say for sure though."

"What about the woman?"

"Police haven't had any hits on her, and I'm still waiting to pilfer the autopsy photos so I can run facial recognition. But if Winston is washed, I don't have high hopes."

"None of this makes sense," Mack said, his fist bouncing against his leg as he paced. "I don't buy that it's unrelated, but he's never dumped a male body before."

"He's never dumped two locked together before either," Mina pointed out. "It makes me wonder if he had to get rid of the body and wanted to throw the cops off so they wouldn't link the two victims to him."

"Possible," Mack said with a head tilt and then paused in his pacing.

"Likely if the man is Little Daddy," Charlotte said, still incredibly aware of Mack's maleness every time he got near her. "If he came up with no past, I'm inclined to believe it's him."

"Me too," Mina agreed. "I'm trying to get an autopsy photo of him to show to Bethany."

"Is that smart?" Mack asked before Charlotte could say anything. "She said she never saw his face."

"The eyes don't lie," Charlotte whispered, and Mina pointed at her through the camera.

"The eyes don't lie. A woman will always recognize the eyes of the person who hurt her."

Mack glanced at Charlotte. She knew what he was thinking, so she smiled. He hadn't hurt her last night. If anything, he healed another little piece of her.

"In the meantime, I found six properties within twenty miles of where the bodies were found that are owned by holding companies. I will send the addresses to your GPS unit."

"Are they rented or empty?" Charlotte asked, grabbing her gun belt from the bed and strapping it on. Mack was insistent that they both be armed, so she had no choice but to wear it today. She still didn't like carrying a gun, but she'd come to realize that sometimes they were necessary to protect those you cared about—and she cared about Mack.

"I'm still trying to get a bead on all of that. For now, approach with caution."

"Affirmative," Mack said, holstering his gun.

"You're not going to approach the houses dressed like that, are you?" Mina asked, her head shaking. "You'll get shot."

"If that's the case, at least we'll know we found the right house." Mack's statement was tongue-in-cheek but didn't make Charlotte feel better. He glanced between the two women and rolled his eyes. "I was kidding. When people see someone dressed in all black with a flak jacket, security logo and a gun, they automatically see you as an authority figure. It might help us get information from neighbors who surround these places."

"Sounds like you have your work cut out for you. I'll stay in touch via your phone. If I call, answer it, no matter what. It could mean life or death depending on what comes through in the next few hours."

"Ten-four. Mike out."

Mina gave a beauty queen wave, and then the screen went black, plunging them into silence. They had to get going if they were going to check out all six houses today. Charlotte grabbed her things and followed Mack to their rental.

"Ready?" Mack asked, straightening her vest. "Remember, head on a swivel and stay behind me until we know the house is empty."

"I got it, Mack," she promised, offering him a smile. Less than two hours ago, they were exploring each other's bodies. He'd been a gentle and patient lover, but she still couldn't give him what he wanted, what he needed. Not in a seedy motel. Her time in places like this one had left scars too deep to overcome last night. She'd helped him reach a satisfying conclusion, but she knew it wasn't how he'd hoped.

"Stop," he whispered, leaning into her ear to kiss it. "What did we talk about this morning?"

"That you have no expectations, and I have the control over any relationship we have."

"And do you believe that, or are you just repeating it back to me?"

She paused for a minute to gaze into his chocolate eyes. "I believe it." He raised a brow. "I believe it." The words were firm and loud. "I believe in you, Mack, and I trust you."

He pulled her to him by her vest and took her lips in a too-short kiss. "Now I believe you. We're in this together, Char. Let's find this killer and return to our lives at Secure One."

"Ten-four, Char out," she said with a wink as she climbed into the car and prepared for battle.

Chapter Nineteen

The first three houses had been a waste of time. There were two without basements, and the third one was rented by a lovely family who was scared to see the "police" arrive. Charlotte had quickly assured them they had done nothing wrong, but after chatting with them, it was easy to see they knew nothing. Mack was frustrated but determined to find the rest of the properties even if it was a waste of time. They'd managed to avoid the actual police, and he was glad the place wasn't crawling with FBI agents. If he had to guess, he'd say the police hadn't tied the two victims to The Red River Slayer, so they hadn't called in the feds. He was starting to think this was a wild goose chase.

A glance at the passenger seat reminded him to trust his gut. Char was, so he'd follow her lead. The couple had gone into the river relatively close to where they were found, considering the time of death. Earlier, they'd parked off the beaten path and used high-powered binoculars to scope out the crime scene. Mack noticed a reedy area that could have trapped the bodies if he'd dumped them in just a little farther upstream. He hoped Mina would get them more information before they had to return for Dorian's party. They had one more night here, two at best, before they'd have to leave for Minnesota.

He slid his gaze to Char for a moment before focusing back on the road. Last night had been special. In his mind, they had made love. Maybe not in the traditional sense, but she had learned to trust him with her body. He always knew baby steps would be required when teaching her about intimacy, and he was okay with that. They were a team, no matter what.

He couldn't help but think how gorgeous she was in the light of the noon sun, but he knew he could never be with her once she healed. Despite the things he told her about healing and hope, none of it applied to him. He would live the rest of his life knowing what he did, but he couldn't ask someone else to live it too. He didn't deserve a family. Not when one died because of his mistakes.

Mack waited for his gut to clench at the thought of that day as it usually did. He waited for another mile but still nothing. He tried to drag the memory up front and center, but all he could see was her curves in the moonlight, and all he could hear was the sound of her moans in his ear.

"You broke the rules." His voice was harsh and needy inside the car, and he cleared his throat. "I told you to stay behind me."

Char rolled her eyes, but he pretended not to notice. "We were approaching a house with a woman and two little kids outside. I didn't want her calling the cops before we could talk to them. Sometimes, you have to know when to lead and when to follow, Mack."

Her sentence was pointed, and then she fell silent. Maybe she could sense the anxiety rolling off him about the case and what happened last night. Would last night change their working relationship once they returned to Secure One? He'd like to say no, but he knew better. He could pretend it didn't affect him, but every time he saw her, he'd know he could never have her. He slammed his palm down on the steering wheel with disgust.

"Everything okay?" Her question was meek and worried, so he forced himself to relax. He didn't want to scare her.

"I'm just frustrated," he said with resignation. "This guy is out there killing people, and we're running all over creation on a wild goose chase."

"We don't know that it's a wild goose chase, and besides, at least we're doing something. That's more than we can say for the authorities. Did they ever get anything out of the guy who tried to kidnap Ella?"

Before he could stop himself, his thumb came up to trace the bruise across the bottom of her chin. The bruising on her face had turned to a sickly yellow as it started to fade, but it never detracted from her beauty.

"No. The guy took his right to remain silent and has done so, but Mina is looking into his background. She has to be careful since Secure One is also wrapped up in that situation."

"Secure One is wrapped up in many situations, it seems."

"We're a security company," he said with a shrug. "It's bound to happen when you have high-profile clients. This won't be the last tangle we have with law enforcement, but we earn our stripes with them by cooperating and working together."

"I thought the feds didn't want us involved in this."

"I'm not talking about the feds. They're entirely different animals as far as cooperation and working together. They don't and won't."

Mack noticed the smirk on Char's face before she spoke.

"I wonder if they know one of their former agents is the one who gets us the information."

"I'm sure they often look the other way regarding what Mina does. Roman figures that they don't come down on her because they can't prove she's hacking their system."

"Mina thinks they feel guilty for what happened with her boss and The Madame."

"That could be too," Mack said on a shrug. "They owe that woman more than they can ever repay her. Besides, they know if anyone can figure out what's going on, it's Mina Jacobs."

"True story," Char said with a smile. "Are we almost to the next place?"

"About two miles out. We have two on this side of Sugarville and one a few miles outside of town. After we stop at these two, we'll look around Sugarville for something to eat and a little information."

"Lunch with a side of snooping. I'm in," she said, throwing him a wink that sank low in his belly and reminded him just how empty his life would be without her.

CHARLOTTE CLIMBED FROM the car and stretched. She'd taken the flak jacket and gun belt off after the last house was nothing more than rubble. She'd put it back on after lunch, but if they wanted to blend in and get information about Bethany or the people in the river, they couldn't look like cops. She eyed Mack as he pumped gas. That was going to be harder for him than for her. Maybe she should take the lead and do the talking.

When they'd pulled into Sugarville, Mack had pointed out the service station as the one Bethany had used the night she ran away. He'd even smiled for the first time all day when he saw the truck parked next to the station. He said Bethany would be pleased to know they got it back. Bethany would be pleased, but Charlotte wasn't. Since they'd climbed out of bed this morning, Mack had been distant and gruff. She tried to tell herself he was just frustrated by the case, but part of her knew that was a lie. Before the sun rose, he had already pulled away from her and climbed back inside his armor.

A warmth slid through her at the thought of their night together. She never intended to fall into bed with him, but their connection was too strong to ignore when they were alone. How he touched, kissed and cared about her spoke volumes about him. Mack wanted to pretend he was hardened by war and unwilling or unable to care about someone now, but that was all it was. Pretending. She knew the war had changed him. Shaped him. Hurt him. But all of that made him more empathetic and in touch with people's emotions. He'd have to come to that realization by himself though.

They walked into the tiny gas station to pay for their fuel. With any luck, they'd learn a bit of information from the attendant as well. A man turned from the back counter when they walked in.

"Welcome to Sugarville Service Center. Find everything you need, folks?"

"Sure did," Mack said with an easy smile. Charlotte noticed he did that whenever they wanted information. She could picture soldier Mack doing the same thing. She'd tell him anything he wanted to know if he flashed that smile at her. "I noticed the old truck by the station. Is that a '61 Ford?"

A grin lit the man's face as he took Mack's money to

cash him out. "Sure is. It's been a workhorse all these years. It was stolen, and I nearly cried when I discovered it was gone. I was never more surprised than when the sheriff from two towns over drove it back to me. It wasn't even damaged."

"Sounds like some kids took it for a joyride."

"Could be. The police said people near where it was abandoned saw a woman get out of it and take off on foot. I tell myself she was in trouble, and the truck got her to safety. That way, I don't get too mad about her stealing it."

Mack dipped his head in agreement, but his gaze slid to Charlotte's for a moment. "I'm glad you got it back." He took his change from the man and motioned outside. "We're looking at some property and heard there was a house for sale up the way here. I'm having difficulty finding it on my GPS though."

The man shook his head for a moment before he spoke. "No houses for sale that I know of unless they're selling the old Hennessy place. Last I heard, it was in probation. No, what's the word?"

"Probate?"

He pointed at Mack. "That's it. Probate. Old man Hennessy died years ago, and nothing has happened with it since. Maybe it is for sale now, but I'm usually the first to know if a place goes up. I wouldn't buy it though."

"Bad water or foundation?" Mack asked, stepping closer as though he were ready for some hot tea to spill.

"Bad juju," he said, looking over Mack's shoulder to the door. "We call it the murder house around here. Someone should have torn it down long ago. Nothing good is going to come from that place. Years ago, a young couple rented the place. Their lives ended in a murder-suicide with a young baby in the house. By the time they found the couple way out there in the woods, the youngster was nearly dead from lack of food and water. It was an ugly scene, but the landlord, old man Hennessy, wouldn't part with the place. He kept saying one day he'd clean it up and sell it. He may have cleaned it up, but he never sold it. He just let it sit empty. I'm still hoping they tear it down. Nothing good comes from land tainted with that kind of violence."

A shiver ran through Charlotte. *Nothing good comes from land tainted with that kind of violence.* Something told her he was right.

THE ALLURE OF a hot meal lured them into the small café. Mack's stomach grumbled from hunger, and he was ready to dive into a plate of whatever the server set in front of him. He wasn't picky. The army had cured him of that. MREs were no joke, and you learned quickly that the hot sauce was there for a reason. Besides, when you're hungry and hunkered down, trying not to get shot, you don't care what you put in your mouth as long as it keeps you alive long enough to escape.

"What did Mina say?" Charlotte asked when they slid into a booth.

"She's looking into it. She said the house is now owned by a holding company, which contradicts what the service station guy said."

"I didn't get too far in school, so I don't know what a holding company does."

The look on her face told him she was embarrassed to admit that, but he was proud of her for asking questions rather than wondering what things meant.

Stop it. You cannot be proud of this woman. She is not yours.

After a firm reminder to himself, he answered her. "A holding company is a business that owns, holds, sells or leases real estate. They get paid multiple different ways depending on the property. If a holding company owns the property in question, there were likely no heirs to leave it to, or the heirs didn't want to deal with the property, so they sold it to a holding company."

"Is it a way to hide properties you don't want people to know you own?"

Mack made the so-so hand. "It takes longer to find the owner, but the information is still there. On the surface, yes, if you don't dig any deeper."

"But Mina will dig to the bottom."

He tossed her a wink as the server approached them to take their order. After ordering a burger and fries with a cold pop, they waited for the server to return with their drinks. Mack had his phone on the bench, awaiting Mina's call or text. He had a bad feeling about this place, and the last thing he wanted was to put Char in the middle of an ambush. He forced his mind to slow and remember that the house was probably crumbling like all the others.

The server brought their drinks and set them down. "Can I get you anything else?"

Mack promptly picked up his glass and took a long swallow, giving Char the chance to jump in. "Actually," she said, holding up her finger. "Do you know anything about the murder house?"

Mack cringed, but rather than shut her down or try to smooth it over, he decided to wait her out. Sometimes shock value was the best value.

"You shouldn't be asking after that place now," the server said in an accent that made Mack smile. "Nothing good gonna come by talking about it."

Charlotte smiled the smile he'd seen before when she was summoning patience from within herself. "We are here to represent the property owners and just wanted to get a feel from the locals before we went out there."

This time Mack opened his mouth to jump in because the last thing he wanted was to have the actual holding company find out someone was impersonating them. He snapped his jaw shut when the server started to speak. After all, they wouldn't be here long enough for anyone to know who they were anyway.

"Oh, I see, ya," she said, putting her hands on her hips. "Well, that place has been empty so long that it should be torn down. Who'd want to live there anyway? Devil worship and rituals, sex rings and murders. I'm glad it's hidden in the woods, so we don't have to look at it."

Mack raised a brow at Charlotte as if to say, *Next question.* She didn't disappoint him.

"Devil worship and sex rings? We knew about the deaths and the poor baby inside the house, but devil worship? You don't say?"

"The seventies were wild times," she said with a shake of her head. "The locals say the pentagram is still on the wooden floor in the living room. Before the owner put up a gate, kids used to go out there huntin' ghosts. The new generation doesn't bother it now, but the stories will be campfire legends forever."

"I see," Charlotte said with a smile. "Thank you for your candidness."

"No problem. Your food will be up in a few minutes."

The waitress turned away, and Mack waited until she had disappeared behind the counter before he leaned in and spoke to Char. "Excellent interrogation. Just be careful about misrepresenting us. We don't want that to roll back on Secure One."

She sipped from her pop, her perfectly pink lips wrapped around the straw, and his groin tightened at the thought of them being wrapped around him. Working with her but not having her was going to be the greatest torture he'd ever been through, and he knew torture.

"We won't be here long enough for anyone to know the truth," she said with a shrug. "A little white lie was warranted. I took a chance."

Mack leaned back in the booth but couldn't wipe the smirk off his face. He was so damn proud of this woman, and no matter how much he told himself not to be, he couldn't help it.

"So now we know there's a gate," she said, pulling him from his thoughts. "How do we plan to get around that?"

"Go in from the backside." His answer was simple, but the execution would be more difficult. "I'm not pulling a rental car up the driveway and hopping a fence. We don't know if they have cameras on the place or a security system. It won't be an easy walk through the woods, but it will give us the advantage of checking out the property before we step foot on it."

"I'm ready," she assured him. "Or I will be after I down that burger and fries. Breakfast left me unsatisfied, but I guess that was my fault. I'll make sure you get a raincheck." She threw in a wink that said she was serious.

Mack groaned, partly at the memory of her body under his hands and partly because he wanted that raincheck more than anything else in this world. He was already on a slippery slope, and making love to her would have him tumbling right into love with her. That couldn't happen.

Chapter Twenty

Charlotte followed Mack through the woods, and the sun filtered down through the heavy overhang of leaves this time of year. Under her feet, the earth was spongy, and with every step, she sank deeper and deeper into the history of this house. If even some of the stories about this house were true, it should be torn down. No one should live in a place with that kind of violence. She stumbled, nearly face-planting on a fallen tree, until Mack grabbed her vest and stopped her fall.

"Careful, sweetheart," he whispered, his voice husky instead of gruff. "I don't want to carry you out of here on a stretcher."

She looked up at him and smiled with a nod before they started moving again. According to his GPS, they should be getting close to the property line. Charlotte could see nothing but trees, leaves and shadows of light and dark. She couldn't deny that she was creeped out being encased in the woods on their way to a murder house. Who wouldn't be?

Mack held up his hand, so she held her position, waiting for him to tell her what to do. He pointed to his right and then motioned to a fallen log. They walked to it and sat, using the log as back support. He pulled out his phone and flipped open the top. It might look like an old-fashioned flip phone, but it was as high-tech as they came. It was text, call and GPS sensors and trackers.

"Has Mina sent more information yet?"

"That's why I stopped. The property is just through those trees, but before we approach, I want to know if there's a security fence."

He opened the text app and read silently for a moment, a heavy sigh escaping as he hit two buttons and then snapped the phone shut.

"Bad news?" she asked, his posture now soldier-straight.

"More like Mina was able to confirm what the waitress said. All of it. The house has been abandoned, and the holding company plans to take it down and sell the land. The couple who lived there were known to be devil worshippers, and the townspeople weren't happy about it. Especially when they found out the couple held rituals on the land and near the river. The police suspect the murder-suicide was staged, but they could never prove it."

"Staged? As in someone else killed them both?"

"Exactly," he said, grasping his lower lip as a shiver went down her spine. "The townsfolk may have had enough and taken them out, shifting the blame to the guy as the shooter."

"It wouldn't be hard to do that, I suppose," Charlotte said. "Disgusting and wrong, but not hard."

"And with a baby in the house," he said, his teeth clenched. He had seen atrocities done to families and children while in the service. Sometimes, the human race angered him beyond words.

"They may not have known the baby was there if it

was sleeping," she mused. "Regardless of all of that, what about a security system?"

"None that Mina could find. There's the gate to stop interlopers and a fence that fell years ago, but no one bothered to repair it. We'll approach with our eyes open and look for signs of recent use before we go in. If I say fall back, you do it. Do not question it. Agreed?"

"Agreed," she said as they stood and stepped over the log, heading for the small knoll that would let them look down on the property before they tried to walk in.

Driving in and parking the car in the driveway would be much simpler but too obvious. Secure One preferred ghost status. If they could get in and out with the information for the team without leaving a trace, it would be worth the long walk through the woods. When they got to the knoll, they rested on their bellies while Mack surveyed the property with his binoculars. They couldn't see a car, but the property was too overrun with vines and leaves to look for tracks from this far away.

"Hey," Charlotte said when he put away the binoculars. "What happened to the kid?"

"Mina hit a dead end with that one. The baby was taken to the hospital, nursed back to health and then adopted. The adoption was closed due to the crime and stigma, so no one knows where the baby ended up." Mack reached for his pants at that moment. "Just got a text." He pulled out the phone and checked it, his brow going up this time while he read. "They identified the woman. Her name is May Rosenburg. She's from Philly. She lived on the streets and had a sheet for minors like theft and prostitution. She was reported missing by a friend about two years ago, but no one has seen her since."

"That means he held her about the same amount of time as Bethany," Charlotte said, her heart in her throat. "Maybe she was the woman who went to Big Daddy when Bethany first arrived. She may have been told by Little Daddy to use a different name, just like Bethany."

"Feels like it. Bethany never saw her face, so it won't help to ask her. The problem is the couple's cause of death."

"They weren't strangled?" she asked, and Mack shook his head.

"No. May had a broken neck and what looked like recent trauma to her body. Chip died of cerebral edema and a head wound."

"If it is The Red River Slayer, something happened that threw him off, and he just had to get rid of the bodies."

"Little Daddy," Mack said with conviction. "I bet he found Little Daddy locked in the room where Bethany left him. Why May would have a broken neck, I can't say."

"If this is him, he's coming apart at the seams, that's why," Charlotte muttered. "Can we go check this place out so we can leave? I don't like the air here."

"Me either." He helped her up so they could start down the hill. "It reminds me of this one time in the sandbox when we were guarding a village. There was a rumor among the locals that a witch put a spell on the town that required bloodshed every twelve and a half days. You felt the blood on the ground under your feet and tasted the copper on your tongue. The evil seeped into your soul. That's what this place reminds me of."

As they approached the house from behind, a cold shiver of dread worked its way down her spine. The place may be empty of souls, but the evil remained. He motioned for her to follow him to the back of the house, where he plastered himself along the door. After looking through the window, he stepped around her, and she followed as he walked to the edge of the house.

"I've seen no cameras, and the kitchen was empty," he whispered as they walked around the side. He paused to peer in every window and ran a hand across his neck before he went to the next one. At the edge of the building, he searched for cameras on the eaves or near the front door. "No cameras on the front of the house. No tire tracks. There's a concrete walkway, so there is no way to check for footprints. Stay tight to the house, and we'll check windows."

She nodded, and they slid around the corner. Mack ducked his head around the edge of the first window and gave her another hand gesture. He pointed for her to stop by the concrete steps leading to the front door. He climbed them quietly and looked through the sheer curtain that hung over the window. He gave her a headshake and a gesture to come around the steps and meet him on the other side. She followed him around the house as he looked in the windows until they got to the back of the house again.

"The house is old and empty. There's a basement, but didn't Bethany say she went out a door in the basement and ran?"

"That's what she said. Is there an old-fashioned cellar door in the yard?" she whispered, afraid to speak at full volume in case they weren't alone.

"I didn't see one, but that doesn't mean it isn't there. We're here. I say we go in."

"Is that smart without backup?" Charlotte asked, her stomach tossing the hamburger and fries around like a blender. Her nerves were taut, and she didn't like the feel of the place.

"No one is around, and Mina is monitoring us on the GPS link. We'll take a quick peek and then head that direction to the river." He pointed straight ahead through the trees from the back of the house. "It can't be far."

"I don't hear the water though."

"It's a slough, so you wouldn't." He pulled out a kit from his vest, but she stopped his hand before he could pick open the door.

"Shouldn't one of us stand guard?"

"In and out. I'll check the basement while you aim your gun at the top of the stairs. Shoot anyone who shows their face because it will be no one good. Got it?"

"Understood," she said and waited while he picked open the door. She understood it, but she didn't like it.

THEY SHOULDN'T BE HERE. The hair on the back of Mack's neck stood up as they crept through the house. It was empty, of that he had no doubt, but the evil permeated the air like a black fog. Mack held up until Charlotte bumped into him. They were walking back-to-back, keeping both exits covered, just in case.

"We're running on the assumption that the basement is clear, but you know what they say about assuming. Can you walk down backward, or do you want me to?"

"I can," she whispered, and he noticed her avert her eyes from the faded pentagram on the floor.

He twisted the knob on the basement and swung his gun down the stairs, the filtered lights from the windows illuminating the floor below. It was finished with worn '70s carpet and smelled of mildew and pine cleaner. It appeared empty. His mind's eye was still stuck on that pentagram as he started the slow and careful trek down the stairs. He swung his gun in both directions of the open stairway, being slow and cautious to ensure Char could keep up with him.

You shouldn't be here.

The warning was louder in his mind this time, and he shook his head, forcing his heart to slow and stop pounding so loudly he couldn't hear his own thoughts. His boots hit the carpet, and he paused, waiting for Char to take her position with her gun aimed at the stairs. He looked right and left, noticing a utility room with a washer, dryer, hot plate and old fridge in avocado-green. It had been new fifty years ago. His trained eye took in the washer and dryer, and he swallowed around the nervousness in his chest. The doors hung open on the machines, and a bottle of laundry soap sat atop one. They had been used recently.

He motioned to Char that he was going down the hallway to the right, and she nodded her agreement but kept her concentration on the stairs. They hadn't found a second set of stairs or a door to the outside, which meant this probably wasn't the house Bethany had been held hostage in, but he wasn't taking any chances until he knew that for sure.

His gun braced on his flashlight, he turned the beam on and aimed it waist height, swinging it left and right to glance in the open doors as he walked down the hallway. The first door was a small room with a bed and nothing else. The carpet was newer, but the bedding was brand new.

He walked to the next room and swung his flashlight inside. It was a bathroom. There was a toilet, shower and vanity. The floral print shower curtain hung open, and he could smell the fancy soaps from the door. He ducked into the room and took a deep breath before he opened the sink cabinet. Feminine supplies were stacked on the bottom, and a nearly silent grunt left his lips. The garbage can was empty, and the shower was dry. No one had been here recently.

Mack swung out the door, and the flashlight beam flashed off a doorknob at the end of the hallway. It wasn't open like the rest of the doors in the basement, which meant it could be a closet or a door leading out of the basement. There was a doormat on the carpet below the door. Not a closet. With his gun pointed ahead, he glanced backward at Char, still braced to shoot with total concentration. Once he checked the last room, he'd see if the other door led to a set of stairs. If it did, he'd grab Char, and they'd follow them to see where they went.

The third room in the hallway was bigger. Mack stepped in and swept his light in an arc. The room was in shambles. Shattered dishes were strewn across the floor, a broken table and a bed with sheets and blankets sliding onto the floor. He could see that the bedding and dishes were modern, which meant they'd been bought long after the appliances.

It's time to leave.

The voice was right, but not before he got solid proof that this house was where Bethany had been held. He walked to the bed and lifted the bedsheets to see lines of four scratches slashed out by a fifth, repeating across the wood in a macabre pattern of desperation. He stood and lowered his flashlight to the floor long enough to get his phone. He'd take a picture, and then they were heading straight to the authorities with what they knew.

He checked the door and then knelt to take the picture, the low light making it difficult, so he set his gun down on the bed and picked up his flashlight. Something tickled his nose, and he sniffed. There was a soft swish of fabric, and he turned, expecting Char. Instead, a crack of pain was followed by encroaching blackness around his head. He fell to the floor and slumped over as the door to the room slammed shut and the lock engaged.

I told you we shouldn't be here.

THE GASOLINE MADE a satisfying sound as it spilled onto the ground around the house. It was time to burn this place down the way it should have been years ago. Was he taking a chance that the rest of the town would go up with it? Sure, but that'd be fine too. Let everyone in this town burn for the sins of their parents. Things were getting a little hot for him here anyway. He chuckled at his joke as he stood in the middle of the yard with the can. He'd allow himself the joy of staging a dramatic scene for the towns-people first. *This would be the most fitting tribute of all though*, he thought as he poured the gasoline, following the lines in his mind to draw the pentagram. It always came back to the blackness in his soul. He couldn't get rid of it. He'd been born with it, and no matter how hard his parents tried, they couldn't cast it out of him. And they'd tried so many times. He had flashbacks to the priest tossing the holy water on him repeatedly until he was dripping wet. He was never saved because he was owned by the darkness, and he would remain there until he died.

He proved that when he killed his parents in broad daylight and tossed them in the river the day he turned eighteen. They were never found, which didn't surprise him, considering where he'd dumped them. The hardest part had been playing the woeful son who didn't know why his parents hadn't returned from vacation. They'd never found their car, and after thirty years, they never would.

The match flared to life, and he tossed it into the middle of the design, the beast inside roaring as the design came to life in flames of beauty. The heat seared his skin, and he took several steps back, watching as it licked and burned until it ran out of fuel to stay alive. He took the can back to the garage and slipped inside, stowing it in the front of the garage where it would only add to the inferno once he touched a match to this piece of his history. People thought him to be so normal and morally upstanding, but they had never seen the beast that lived within him. They had, but they didn't know those women in the river were offerings from the beast himself.

One final walk down these steps, and he'd say goodbye to the piece of his childhood that had shaped him as a man. This house had nearly killed him, but in the end, it had offered him so much life. He would miss it, but he had to go underground for a bit until he knew where that woman ended up. A shame. He had just gotten into a rhythm too.

A beam of light flashed under the door, and he froze on the third stair from the bottom. It flicked across the door two more times before it disappeared. He wasn't alone. The game had just changed, but no matter who waited on the other side, they'd perish in a fire hotter than the bowels of hell.

CHARLOTTE CONCENTRATED ON the stairs, but it wasn't without difficulty. Mack had disappeared down the hallway what felt like an eternity ago. It probably hadn't been more than a few minutes, but she slid a glance to her right without moving her gun. She caught his vest as he disappeared into the final room at the end of the hall. They had to get out of here. She could feel it in her bones. The scent of laundry detergent and cleaner filled her head, telling her someone had been here recently.

A door slammed, and she swung her arm in an arc toward the sound. "Mack?"

The response was a guttural roar as a figure ran at her from the end of the hallway. It wasn't Mack. The man's face was twisted into a mask of horror, his hands out, ready to grasp her neck and take her down. The gun went off, the bullet striking him in the shoulder, but it barely slowed him down. Three more shots rang out in the basement, the sound echoing around the cement until she was sure she would never hear anything again. The man stumbled and then fell to his knees at her feet.

Charlotte gasped when he gazed up at her. With the mask gone, she knew the man sitting before her. He was a United States senator. He fell to his side, one hand gripping his chest as blood poured from his wounds.

She kept her gun aimed at him while she screamed Mack's name. When she got no response, she gazed at the man before her. "What did you do to him?"

He gasped, and blood bubbled up around his lips. "Help me," he muttered, gripping his belly where more blood oozed over his fingers.

Charlotte grabbed her cuffs and attached one of his ankles to the stair railing. He wasn't going anywhere in his condition, and she had to help Mack. She jumped over his writhing body and ran to the room at the end of the hallway, but the door was locked when she tried to turn the knob. "Mack!" she screamed, throwing her shoulder into the door without it budging. She ran back to the man on the floor. "Where's the key?"

Greg Weiss smiled at her, his teeth stained pink from the blood bubbling out of his lips. He spat at her. "Go to hell."

"I've already been there because of men like you," she growled, placing her foot on his gut and pressing until he howled in pain the way her soul had wanted to for years. She dug in his pockets until she found a key ring and gave him one solid kick to remember her by before she ran back to the closed door, her boot leaving a blood print on the carpet every other step.

Her fingers weren't cooperating, and she fumbled with the keys while Weiss howled. The sound had changed. It was no longer pain. It was anger and the fading light of a man who had taken souls that were now driving him down into hell where he belonged. The key went into the lock, and she flipped it, the door opening to reveal the man she loved. The thought nearly sent her to her knees, but she couldn't take the time to stop. She had to help him.

"Mack!" she screamed again, running to him and sliding to a stop next to where he lay crumpled on the carpet. "Mack," she cried, checking for a pulse. It was strong and steady, but that gave her only a modicum of relief. He was alive but unconscious, and they needed to get out of the house. Charlotte lifted his head onto her lap and noticed a spot on his head that was matted and bloody. "Come on, Mack," she cried, slapping his face gently to wake him.

The man in the other room had quieted other than an occasional moan and stream of cuss words sent her way. Charlotte hoped he lived so everyone could see the monster he was.

"Mack," she whispered, kissing his soft warm lips. "Please, Mack, wake up. I need your help. I don't know what to do." She begged him to wake up, kissing him over and over until she left her lips on his, and tears ran down her cheeks. "I love you, Mack Holbock. You can't do this to me." Her tears fell silently until a hand came up to hold her waist. She started but realized it was Mack's warm hand holding her hip.

"Char," he whispered until she met his pained gaze. "Slayer."

Weiss took that moment to cuss her out again, and Mack's lips tipped up in a smile. "He's been neutralized," she promised, rubbing his cheek.

"Who is it?" he managed to ask, putting his hand to the side of his head by the wet spot.

"You won't believe me, but it's Senator Greg Weiss."

"Call Mina. Now."

Charlotte grinned and lifted the phone from his pants pocket. "No need to rush. He's got four of my bullets in him, and they all had a woman's name on them. He's not going anywhere other than hell."

She flipped the phone open and hit the call button while Mack grinned. "Sweetheart, I love you too."

His eyelid went down in a wink as she heard, "Secure two, Whiskey."

That was when she knew they were finally safe.

Epilogue

Charlotte closed the sketchbook with a sigh. It had been a week since they had unknowingly ended the reign of terror The Red River Slayer had had over the country. When the news broke that Senator Greg Weiss was fighting for his life in surgery as the suspected slayer, the media converged on the little town of Sugarville like the vultures they were. Charlotte didn't care. She was already in Cal's plane after Mack was treated and released from a hospital for his head laceration.

Weiss had used a weapon of convenience and hit Mack with a piece of the broken table he had killed Little Daddy with just a few days before. According to his confession, Weiss had pushed May down the stairs, which resulted in a broken neck and her death. To throw the authorities off, he wrapped May in Little Daddy's arms and tossed them in the river as a red herring. If the authorities were busy concentrating on a new twist to the case, he had time to disappear.

First, Weiss had to destroy the evidence. He planned to burn down the old house, but Char and Mack had beat him to the property. Had they been thirty minutes later, the house and the evidence would have been gone.

As it turned out, Little Daddy was one of the senator's

"staffers." The only thing he staffed was the senator's deranged house of horrors. He trained the women to be the senator's "assistant."

The fact that no one on Capitol Hill questioned his turnover of assistants or his story of where the last one went was concerning, but that was above her pay grade. It was good that Bethany had never been transferred up as his assistant because she wouldn't have kept his secret the way the other women had. They believed that he would take care of them forever and be their sugar daddy if they did his bidding. Bethany knew better.

Greg survived his surgery, but one of her bullets had hit his spine, and he would never walk another day in his life. When the police deposed him with a list of his suspected crimes and the threat of life in prison without parole looming over his head, he asked for a deal. He knew he would never survive in the general population in a wheelchair, so there was little choice. He sang like a canary, documenting his killings on a timeline that shocked even the seasoned FBI agents. It started, he said, when he found out that his birth parents had been killed by Christian conservatives in their house and left him there to die. He swore that he sold his soul to the devil for the chance to avenge their deaths. Adopted by a loving family in Maine, he had a charmed life on the surface, but underneath simmered a monster so evil that Charlotte wasn't convinced anyone was safe until he was dead, no matter how many doors they locked him behind.

And then he died.

The nurses walked in one morning to find him dead in bed. An autopsy revealed he threw a clot, and it went to his heart. Good riddance was Charlotte's first thought.

Her second thought was she was the one to bring closure and justice to the families of his victims. Sure, some of his victims had no family, but that didn't mean they didn't deserve justice. Before he died, he'd signed the confession and accepted the title of The Red River Slayer.

A shudder went through her, and warm hands came up to grasp her shoulders. "Hey, you okay?" Mack asked from near her ear.

"Fine," she promised, shaking off the evil of a man who no longer walked the earth. "I was just finishing a sketch. How are things in the control room? I know I caused Cal a huge headache."

"No, you saved my life and the lives of countless other people by killing that monster. A little time and money are nothing in the scheme of things. You can always make more money but you can't bring people back to life."

Her sigh was heavy, and she nodded, not making eye contact with him. They hadn't discussed their adrena-line-driven declaration of love since it happened, and she wasn't sure they ever would. She promised herself she would wait for him to bring it up again, but so far, he'd remained mum. "Do you have a minute? I was wondering if I could give you something."

Mack walked around the table and perched on a stool. "Sure, what's up?"

With her heart pounding, she opened her sketch pad and pulled out the loose sheet waiting there. She slid it across the table and waited while he gazed at it.

"The real-me sketch," he whispered, running his finger across her signature at the bottom. "That's what I call it in my head," he explained, lifting his gaze to make eye contact with her.

"You said you'd like to have it when and if I was ready to give it to you. Is that still the case?"

"Absolutely," he said, drawing it nearer as though she may take it back. "I love that you signed it Hope."

"That's what you've given me, Mack. You gave me hope back that first night I was here, and you've continued to offer it over and over until I was strong enough to believe that I deserve it."

"You do deserve it, Char. You became my hope the moment you walked onto this property."

"Do I deserve your heart too, or is that not on the table?" she asked, fear making the words shake. "I'm sorry for asking, but I have to know—"

His finger stopped her words, and he stood in front of her, his forehead touching hers. "My heart is yours if you think you can also accept my ghosts."

"I'll carry yours if you carry mine. Sharing will make them lighter."

He didn't wait. He kissed her with the love of a man who finally had what he needed in life. "I'm so thankful for you, Char," he whispered when the kiss ended. "I didn't know how to come to you and ask, so I prayed you'd come to me. Mina called me a chicken and a coward. In fairness, I agreed with her."

Her laughter was soft, but there were tears of pain, fear, acceptance and hope in the sound. "Mina is never afraid to call it as she sees it."

"And I always will," Mina said from behind them. "I'm glad you two finally figured yourselves out before we formed a Secure One intervention."

Mack grabbed Charlotte when she tried to pull away and kissed her neck. "You're ruining our moment, Whiskey."

"Sorry, but you'll have to save that moment for later when you're alone. We've been summoned to the conference room. There are updates to the case."

Charlotte had to admit that she was curious, so she followed Mack to the conference room where the team had gathered. Cal was at the front and motioned for Charlotte and Mack to sit in the empty seats. Eric, Selina, Roman and Efren had rounded out the table.

"Efren," Charlotte said with a smile. "Good to see you again."

"You'll be seeing more of him," Cal said. "He's agreed to sign on as another security member for Secure One. We're growing, and we need the help." Selina rolled her eyes with a huff but said nothing else. Cal handed Efren a security badge. "Everyone, welcome Tango to the team."

"Tango. Because I have two left feet?" he asked with a raised brow.

"The way I hear it, you have at least four, but you have to admit, it's the perfect call sign for you," Mina said with a wink.

"I'll accept it, as long as dancing isn't required."

"I can't promise that," Cal said. "As a bodyguard, you may have to take one for the team if your subject has to attend a ball, but we'll try to keep it to a minimum."

The team offered him some good-natured ribbing, minus Selina, who sat mute, her arms crossed over her chest. The moment she'd heard that The Red River Slayer had been taken down, Selina transferred Bethany to a hospital. She was undergoing treatment for her physical conditions as well as her mental health. Bethany had a long road ahead of her, but Charlotte had every intention of being there to help her. Maybe Cal would offer to let her finish her recovery at Secure One when she was released from the treatment facility. Something about the land and the people here healed broken hearts and minds.

After a few moments, Cal brought the room to attention. "As you know," he began, "Weiss confessed before his death, and I was able to obtain a copy of the confession." He glanced at Mina, who was smirking but said nothing. "Mina, would you like to take over?"

She stood and leaned on the table as she stared down Marlise and Charlotte. "Before The Madame set up shop in Red Rye, Greg was killing people sporadically and weighing them down in lakes and rivers where the chance they'd be found again was slim. He killed his adoptive parents and anyone else who got in his way. Then his childhood summer camp friend, Liam Albrecht, called him from Red Rye to tell him about a new escort service in town. Since Liam was on the *special practice date committee*—" which she put in quotation marks "—he funneled women that The Miss wasn't happy with to Weiss. He kept them in the house and used them, but that was when he came up with the idea of dropping them in rivers to make it look like the serial killer was targeting politicians. What he was doing was satisfying his sick fantasies."

"The early women were from The Madame's house in Red Rye?" Marlise asked, and Mina nodded.

"Hard to confirm, but since their identities were washed, we know they were women from within The Madame's empire, no matter what house they lived in."

"And he went underground when The Madame was arrested?" Charlotte asked.

"He never stopped killing. He just didn't showcase the

bodies. We know now that the woman in Arizona stuck in the dam was Emilia. According to the confession, he joined the committee for the waterways in order to throw the cops off his tracks by making the killings look political. That's why he made sure the bodies of those he killed during the two-year break weren't found immediately."

"So he purposely drove to other states with women to dump them in rivers?" Mack asked.

"According to his confession, he transported the women to the river, killed them while they were underwater to make the police think they drowned and then dressed them before their final journey downstream. He claimed in the confession that Layla was a sacrificial lamb, his words," she said, holding her hands up. "May, the woman found with Little Daddy, was a good assistant, and since Layla was untrainable, he killed her specifically to coincide with Ella's party. He was a sick, sick man, and the twenty-page typed confession will take a long time to get through. The point is there was no doubt he was the man behind the slayings."

A shiver settled down Charlotte's spine at the thought, and it was as though Mack knew because his warm hand rubbed it away. "I'm sorry for the trouble my part in this caused you, Cal."

"No," Cal said firmly. "You were the hero that day, Charlotte. Scum like that should eat the bullet of a person they wronged, in my opinion. He may not have held you hostage, but he was responsible for the deaths of so many women in your same situation."

"We couldn't agree more," a voice said from the back of the room. Everyone turned, and Senator Dorian and Ella stood in the doorway.

"Ella!" Charlotte exclaimed, grabbing the young woman as she ran to her for a hug. "I'm sorry I didn't get back to the house after everything."

"I missed you, but I'm so glad you're okay," Ella said, hugging her tightly.

They'd had to postpone the senator's reelection party when he was called back to Washington to deal with the fallout from Weiss's arrest. The party had been rescheduled for next weekend, and Charlotte was looking forward to spending more time with Ella.

She joined her father at the side of the table and squeezed Charlotte's hand. "I just wanted to thank the woman who saved my daughter from a murderer. When Weiss died, the man in custody admitted that Weiss had hired him to kidnap my daughter and take her to the murder house. If you hadn't been there to stop him that night…" He waved his hand around in the air. "I don't even allow myself to think about it. I just know I owe you a debt of gratitude."

"I'm glad she's safe," Charlotte said, embarrassed by the attention. She preferred to stay in the background. "I still intend to give you those drawing lessons, Ella."

"Maybe you can get a few in later this year when you fly to DC to accept an award for your exemplary bravery and service to your country," Dorian said, putting his arm around his daughter.

"What now?" Charlotte asked as everyone else around the table smirked. "DC? Award? Not necessary."

"I will pass your opinion on to the president, but I'm certain he will not feel the same."

"The—the president?" Charlotte stuttered, and Ella was the one to laugh.

"He's the guy who sits in that oval room and runs the country."

Charlotte snorted and put her hand on her hip. "Please, no. That's... No. I was doing my job."

"Technically, you weren't," Cal said from the front of the room. "Your job is to cook, but you were a soldier that day. You didn't hesitate to protect your fellow soldier, even if that protection was driven by love rather than brotherhood."

Charlotte's face heated as Cal handed her a box. She lifted the lid off, and inside was a badge like the one she wore in the Secure One control room. This one didn't say Charlotte though. It said *Public Liaison, Secure One, Hotel*. She glanced up at Cal. "No. I can't take Hotel. My name starts with *C*." Mack rested his hand on her shoulder, which calmed her instantly.

"You can, and you will," Cal said with a smile. "I'm Charlie, so we had to pick a different call name for you. Mack told me that you went by Hope on the streets. In my opinion, Hotel is fitting, and I know Hannah would approve. I hold wonderful memories of her in my heart, but I'm with my soulmate now," he said, winking at Marlise. "Hannah would be proud to share her call name with a woman of your caliber."

Charlotte nodded, tears pricking her eyes as she looped the badge around her neck. "I'll wear the name proudly then. I don't know anything about being a public liaison though. Also, you guys realize I was terrified, and my knees shook the whole time I was in that basement. I think you might be taking things a bit far."

Mack chuckled from behind her as Cal shook his head. "I've never gone into battle and not been terrified with my knees shaking. I don't think anyone around this table has either." Heads shook to the negative until Cal spoke again. "Regardless, you did what had to be done. That's what makes you a soldier and a hero. As for the new job title, we'll talk about that tomorrow."

"Now," Dorian said, motioning toward the door. "There's a whole host of goodies waiting for us in the dining room, and I'm starving!"

Everyone offered congratulations, hugs and laughter before slowly working their way out of the conference room. Charlotte was at the door when an arm looped around her waist and held her back.

"Hold up, Hotel," Mack whispered in her ear. "I need a moment."

Charlotte swung around and draped her arms around his neck. "You can have a moment anytime, Mike."

"Good, because I'm low on hope and need a refill."

"I'm not sure I know how to refill your hope," she quipped, her brow dipping. "Maybe you better give me directions."

"Now that I can do," he promised before he dropped his lips to hers.

* * * * *

There are more books in Katie Mettner's
Secure One *miniseries coming soon!*

*And if you missed the previous
titles in the series, look for:*

Going Rogue in Red Rye County
The Perfect Witness

*Available now wherever
Harlequin Intrigue books are sold!*